CHARLOTTE'S NEMESIS

A COZY MYSTERY IN THE WILDERNESS

Liz Turner

Contents

Chapter 1
A Plot is Hatched

The sleepy lodge laid nestled between trees. Lights blinked through the cabin windows, and a wisp of smoke trailed up into the sky, whispering of the warmth and life that existed inside. The dying rays of the violent red sunset bled on the glossy waters of Lake Athabasca.

"It's rather beautiful, isn't it?" a thick voiced, and equally thick-skulled man said to another.

The two leered out from behind the pine trees skirting the clearing around the lodge.

"Don't be an idiot, Denver." The darker-haired man snarled at his friend. "We're here to do a job and you're distracted by the sunset."

"Why do you always have to do that?" Denver complained, his wide brown eyes fixed on the enormous man next to him.

"Do what?" the man grumbled.

"Talk down at me. And don't shake your head like that, like you don't know what I'm talking about. You do it all the time, Louis. *All* the time."

Louis rolled his eyes and wiped his face down with a hand the size of a plate. He held back the comment that sprang to his lips about it simply being because of a height issue.

"I have feelings, you know," Denver said, his arms folding defensively in front of his chest. His bottom lip poked outward.

Louis scowled, his dark eyes firing darts at the sensitive man who was his partner. Denver was short, stocky, and mean in a fight. But for some bizarre reason beyond Louis's understanding, Denver had a soft heart. "You should leave your feelings behind when we're on a job. We're here to kill a man, and you choose *this* moment to tell me I don't care enough about you?!"

The birds perched in the tree above them launched into the sky, squawking in protest at the disturbance from the men beneath their tree.

"Look what you've done." Denver pointed to the sky. "You've gone and lost your temper again and nearly given away our position!"

Louis attempted to regain control of his breathing. It only took ten minutes on a stakeout with Denver—especially after a long hike through the rough, Northern Canadian forest—to spike his blood pressure.

"I thought you were seeing a counselor for your anger management?" Denver prodded.

"My counselor is none of your darn business!" Louis exploded. More birds took off in alarm. "I swear, I'm going to kill *you* tonight instead of Bill," he threatened between gritted teeth. Bulging veins pulsated in his biceps as he clenched his fists.

"Well, that hurts my feelings," Denver said in a huff.

Louis snapped his teeth down on his tongue to regain control of his temper. They had a job to do, and if they returned to Rick Neilson without their assignment complete, he would have far bigger problems than Denver's tender emotions. "Let's just focus on the task at hand. Which one is Bill's cabin?"

Denver scanned each cabin. "Those look a bit nicer, so I'm guessing they're for the guests."

"Yes, I figured out that much from the large sign that says, 'Guest Cabins'." Louis sighed. He didn't understand why Rick insisted they both come. Bill was an ancient, decrepit coward who couldn't conceivably put up a fight. Meanwhile, this place was run by a woman and some children. Taking Bill out was a one-man job.

"There he is." Denver pointed again. The creak of a cabin door had alerted Denver to the porch where an old man had stepped out.

Bill stood, one hand holding a lantern and the other supporting his tired back. His bearded face gazed up at the emerging evening stars dotting the violet sky.

"He's alone," Louis observed in a hushed whisper. "Let's move in."

Bill seated himself on his porch and placed his feet up on the banister. The cool evening air carried the bite of early autumn, which caused him to draw his coat tighter around him. He slurped from his coffee mug and stooped over to set it down on the floor next to his chair. As he straightened up, he jolted in surprise to see an intimidating figure in front of him.

"Hello, Bill," the man hissed before drawing back his fat fist and spearing it into Bill's face.

Bill, along with his chair, reeled over backwards. A stray boot sent Bill's coffee mug flying, raining a spray of scalding liquid over the two attackers.

Denver yowled and rubbed his eyes.

"Quiet! Grab him," Louis hissed. "We must drag him into the woods and finish the job there. You've already made too much noise here."

Denver hauled the unconscious old man, dragging him towards the stairs. Bill's nose had broken, and blood streamed down his front as his head lolled against his chest.

"Going somewhere?" a voice interrupted.

Louis spun round, every muscle in his rippling body on high alert. When he saw where the voice had come from, he let out a brainless guffaw. "Hey, little lady." He winked at the woman standing in their path. "It's safer for you to walk away."

She had wavy brown hair, soft brown eyes, and looked like a little-person compared to the bulking men towering over her. Regardless, she stood defiantly in their way, her shoulders squared and her chin stubbornly pointed upward.

She raised a rifle and aimed at one man.

Yet, Louis's smirk didn't falter. "Put the weapon down and no one gets hurt," he said, reaching for his own weapon tucked in his belt.

The woman ignored him, took aim, and fired an inch from Louis's foot. Shards of wood splintered from the porch step, and the enormous man practically leapt onto the roof of the cabin.

"You missed," Denver pointed out with a laugh.

"No, I didn't," the woman sneered. "Put the old man down, or I'll start taking out toes."

Denver held his ground and Louis, having recovered from his initial fright, returned to offer support. Toes, they could live without.

"All right, if toes don't scare you…" The woman took a deep breath and in one swift motion re-aimed her weapon, leveling it on Louis's chest. "Drop your gun and kick it over here."

Louis was the larger of the two. By the woman's estimation, he seemed more likely to lunge at her, whereas the shorter, blonder man was weighed down with the unconscious Bill.

"I'm getting nervous, Louis," Denver stammered, raising Bill so he could shield his own torso with the old man's.

"Shut up!" Louis shouted. He then carefully pulled his weapon from his own belt. "And don't use my name, you idiot!" He slowly lowered his weapon to the ground. In the last second, his arrogant smirk alerted the woman to his foolhardy plan of firing at her.

She rolled her eyes and held her breath as she steadied her weapon to fire again, bracing the butt of the gun against her shoulder. One eye closed, she pulled the trigger and grinned in satisfaction as the bullet skimmed past the larger man, ripping his shirt and tearing through the outer layer of skin.

Louis screamed in rage, his hand slapping onto his injured bicep. "You shot me!" he screamed in disbelief, his voice a high-pitched squeak.

"Easy target, all those muscles," she retorted ruthlessly. "I'm only going to ask one more time. Drop the old man and get out of here. She reloaded and raised her rifle to her chin once again. "You're trespassing and I have every right to defend my family."

Denver released Bill. The old man crumpled to the ground, unharmed. Denver then hurried over to his wounded friend and pulled him away from the fight.

"You'll regret this," Louis snarled at her over his shoulder, blood trickling between his fingers.

The woman kept her gun aimed at them until they were safely out of sight, their figures disappearing into the gloomy night.

"Charlotte," the old man cried, his hand reaching up to touch his injured face.

"I'm here, Bill." Charlotte dropped to her knees beside him. "You look like you took a nasty hit to the face."

"My nose is broken again," he gurgled, spitting out a mouthful of blood.

"I know." Charlotte grimaced as she used her fingers to reset his nose. "Sorry, I know that hurt, but at least it's not broken badly."

Bill silently wept from the pain. "Thank you," he spluttered.

"Did you know those guys?" Charlotte asked, helping him into his chair.

His silence answered the question. "Don't tell Oliver, please," Bill pleaded after a moment.

Chapter 2
Family Feud

Charlotte Bouchard, along with her husband, Oliver, were the proud owners and managers of one of the most spectacular remote fishing lodges in Northern Canada. Perched on the edge of the vast waters of Lake Athabasca, their hand-built lodge attracted appreciative thrill-seeking fishers from across the world.

Charlotte felt a flitter of nerves mingled with excitement as an airplane engine roared right above them. It was Nick's signal that he was about to take the plunge and land his metallic bird afloat in the tranquil lake waters. Charlotte readied her well-trained staff for the arrival of a family from Chicago.

"Is the champagne chilled?" she asked a waitress who was bustling past.

"Yes, Charlie. The champagne is in the ice bucket at the welcome buffet," she replied.

"Are the chocolate-coated strawberries—"

"The strawberries are complete," a tall man with dark hair and fierce eyebrows said. "But I'll keep them in the refrigerator until the last moment."

"Thank you, Chef Victor." Charlotte smiled as she approached the large table with the chef. In the center was an impressive arrangement of wildflowers surrounded by an appetizing array of finger snacks that would lure even the fussiest eaters. "You've really outdone yourself, Victor. The eclairs look perfect. And your mini-meat pies have my mouth watering."

"The best for the best, right?" he said.

"You're nervous too, aren't you?" she asked quietly, not wanting the rest of her staff to pick up on her concerns.

"Well, he is a very important politician, isn't he?" Victor rubbed his hands together. "It's not like he has the potential to ruin my career after a single complaint or anything…"

"Yes, he is important." Charlotte habitually chewed her bottom lip. "He's apparently taking a quick break from his campaign to focus on his family life. But I wouldn't worry about your career. You're the best I know."

"Explains why they've chosen such a remote place," the chef said, ignoring Charlotte's compliment. "No press, no reporters, and a safe quiet spot to relax."

"That's true," Charlotte realized. "I actually feel better knowing that our humble little lodge is exactly what they need."

The chef raised an eyebrow before disappearing back into his kitchen. Charlotte wondered if he'd heard the gunshots the night before.

"Here they come," Charlotte announced, spotting a flash of white material through the tree line.

The staff assembled themselves on the front steps wearing welcoming smiles.

Charlotte's chest burned inside, and she realized she'd been holding her breath for the last minute. She let it out slowly and breathed in some fresh air before reapplying her professional grin.

The guests approached slowly. Alf Columbus was a tall, broad-shouldered man in his late forties. His face was a deep shade of plum and he wore a fiercely unhappy expression.

"Oh dear," Charlotte muttered.

"Hang in there," Madison, her friend and manager, comforted her. "They're just ordinary people and this is an above-ordinary lodge."

"Wow, Madi. 'Above ordinary'? We've reached new heights today…"

"Sorry," Madison whispered, her smile faltering. "I always say the wrong thing."

"That you do," Rebekah, the chief housekeeper and tutor for the kids, mumbled.

"Don't start," Charlotte cautioned the two competitive women. "The last thing we need is a feud on our hands."

Charlotte fixed her eyes on the wife—Barb Columbus. She was tall and elegantly dressed, a designer handbag of sorts draped fashionably from her skinny wrist. A silk scarf covered her hair, and she peered disapprovingly over the brim of her sunglasses as she neared the lodge.

"She looks fancy," Madison stated with a mocking snort.

This comment was met with giggles from Rebekah.

"Behave," Charlotte cautioned. "Just because there are no unmarried men for the two of you to fight over doesn't mean you need to channel that unused energy into judging our guests."

Madison and Rebekah scowled but remained silent.

"Look," Thomas piped, "they have a kid!"

Charlotte noticed a shorter figure trudging behind the couple. It was a young girl with a head of sweeping blonde hair that reached her waist. She wore a pretty dress paired with an ugly expression. Charlotte looked down at her fourteen-year-old son, who had never had much exposure to teenage girls.

His expression said it all. They were in for trouble.

"Remember, she's a guest, son," Charlotte scolded.

"She looks like she could use a friend though," Thomas said, his eyes wide.

Charlotte's heart melted. Her son had to be one of the most observant, kind-hearted kids his age. Though she realized—after casting a second glance at the posh-looking, snobby teenage girl—that Tom's heart was one easily broken.

"Tom's in love," Owen crooned at his older brother, mimicking a soppy face.

"Shut up, Owen," Thomas retorted.

Amelia, Charlotte's six-year-old, started giggling, which spread contagiously through the nervous staff.

Charlotte tried desperately to silence them all, but a ferocious glance from Mr. Columbus assured her, without doubt, that they'd heard her misbehaved staff's laughter.

"I apologize," Charlotte began with a warm, reassuring smile as she stepped forward from the group, "but one child said something funny. Uhm… Anyhow, welcome to our lodge." Charlotte beamed a perfect smile. "We're thrilled to have you here."

Alf sneered at her. "That pilot of yours is dreadful. It worried me they had hired him to have us assassinated, at the rate he took that landing."

Charlotte threw a disapproving look at their reckless pilot, Nick. He was currently hidden behind the weighty mountain of the Columbus family's expensive luggage.

"Nick believes it's part of the experience of being in untamed nature," Charlotte said, attempting to lighten the mood. "But we'll have a word with him before you fly out."

"I should hope so," the man continued. "If I had known, I would have used my own private plane."

Nick glowered at his shoes and shook his head with disapproval in the background.

Charlotte jerked her head to the side to signal that he was free to leave for a drink at the bar to recover from the journey he'd endured. It was a rare occasion when Nick wasn't beaming an infectious grin. Hence, Charlotte deduced that the journey must have been desperately unpleasant for all aboard.

"Mrs. Columbus," Charlotte turned to the woman, "I do hope you enjoyed the scenery on your way in."

"Yes, it is rather beautiful, I must admit," she said in a timid voice. "But it alarmed me to see that there are no shopping centers nearby—or cities..."

"Wasn't that the point of this whole stupid trip?" her husband spat. "To get away from all of that and 'be in nature'?"

Mrs. Columbus's cheeks flushed a deep red beneath her heavy make-up, and she pursed her rouged lips. "Well, perhaps if you cared enough about your own family, you would have helped me choose somewhere to go and we wouldn't have ended up in the middle of nowhere!" she snapped back.

Out of the corner of her eye, Charlotte noticed her entire staff dissolve into thin air, trailing away and busying themselves with anything to distract from the awkward atmosphere looming over the Columbus family.

"I do care about my family!" he exploded, a purple vein throbbing in his temple. "That's why I allowed you to drag me out here! So I can scream in peace!"

"If you'd like to follow me," Charlotte interrupted the tirade, bellowing over Alf, "we have an assortment of snacks and chilled champagne for you to enjoy."

"Alcohol is exactly what I need!" the man yelled, storming up the steps.

As he barked at Madison to direct him to the bar, Charlotte took a deep breath, summoned a smile, and focused her attention on Barb Columbus.

"I apologize if things aren't quite up to the city standard your family must be used to, but I hope that you will—"

"Oh hush." The woman waved her hand. "This isn't your fault, darling. My husband is under a lot of stress with all the campaigns and public speeches. It takes a toll."

"I can only imagine. We've prepared some relaxing activities for you to enjoy together as a family," Charlotte continued in a hurry. Her heart was pounding, and she was sweaty at the prospect of having another fight break out.

"Really, what we need is a marriage counselor," Barb continued. "But Alf would never approve. He believes there's nothing wrong with our family. And poor Lola just needs a friend to talk to."

"Mother!" the girl screeched. "I've told you a million times not to discuss the family in public."

"Hi, my name is Thomas."

Charlotte bit her lip as she heard the timid words escape her brave son's mouth. She watched in horror as Lola turned her piercing blue-eyed gaze on the innocent Thomas.

"What?" the girl snarled.

"Uh…" Thomas hesitated, having never experienced peer hostility before.

Charlotte hid her face behind her hand as she noticed the similarities between her son and a helpless lamb moments before slaughter.

"I said that my name is Thomas. I hoped that I could show you around the lodge," he continued, oblivious to Lola's scathing expression.

"I don't want to look around your stupid lodge. I just want to go to my room until this whole stupid holiday is over!"

"Lola, dear," Barb interrupted, "there's no need to throw a tantrum. Why not go for a walk with the friendly boy? He obviously likes you."

Charlotte cringed to her core as her son's cheeks redden with embarrassment. He stuttered through a few unintelligible words before bolting away.

"Now look what you've done!" Lola shouted. "You and Father ruin everything!" She stormed into the lodge.

Charlotte's brain threw up blanks when she tried to think of how to remedy the situation.

"I suppose the cat's out the bag—claws, teeth, and all," Barb said. "We're here to try to save our family. As you can see, we desperately need to figure something out. We can't spend a minute in the same room without screaming at each other."

Charlotte noticed, for the first time, a touch of sincerity in Barb's voice. It tinged her brown eyes with sadness and embarrassment. Charlotte thought Barb might cry, but the stiff woman sniffed and shook her head, as if to stop the well of emotion she couldn't bear feeling any longer.

"Don't give up," Charlotte said. "There's always a way through these things."

Charlotte couldn't explain the powerful urge she felt to help the Columbus family. Perhaps the fact that her own family life was so wonderful made her want to help another experience the same joy.

"Easy for you to say," the woman scoffed. "You don't have a family like mine to deal with."

"That's true. Every family has its own problems though," Charlotte said. "But my husband and I have found that openly communicating about our feelings and problems helps prevent a lot of difficulty later."

"Open communication is practically impossible in my home. Open fighting, yes. That we're good at." Barb gave a harsh laugh. "But actually talking to each other is out of the question."

"Charlie!" a voice yelled.

"Oh, Oliver, hi, this is—"

"Don't, *'Oh, hi Oliver,'* me!" he yelled.

Charlotte's eyes widened in shock. Oliver rarely raised his voice, let alone lose his temper—especially not in front of guests. "What's going on?" she asked while trying to signal with her eyes that they should take their conversation elsewhere.

"When were you planning on telling me we had two thugs trying to take out Bill last night?"

"Oh…" Charlotte swallowed. "I mean, I assumed you heard the gunshots and that Bill would have mentioned something…"

"Bill is not my wife! *You* are! And as your husband, I need to know when you decide to take the law into your own hands and shoot criminals off our property! I thought you were getting rid of stray wolves!"

Charlotte glanced at Barb, who seemed to eat up their family feud. It was apparent that Barb rarely enjoyed the role of spectator in public fights, and she was lapping up every moment.

"Love, perhaps we should discuss this later, in private," Charlotte suggested quietly.

"Open communication, Charlie. That's what we pride ourselves on!" Oliver reminded her, the hurt clear in his eyes. "I don't want to have to find things out from other people. Anyway," he sighed, his evaporating rage leaving him spent, "we can continue this conversation later."

And with that, he was gone.

"So," Charlotte exhaled slowly, "that was my husband, Oliver. As you can see, we still have a few things to work on ourselves."

Barb gave a smug smile and patted Charlotte roughly on her shoulder. "There, there, Mrs. Bouchard, don't give up."

Chapter 3
Heated Words

"What's gotten into you?" Charlotte asked her husband. "It's not like you to scream at me in front of guests."

"I know." He sank his face into his hands. "I was just so angry when I heard that you'd been in danger."

"I wasn't in danger," Charlotte assured, seating herself next to him and wrapping an arm around his shoulders. "I just kind of stumbled across it accidentally. Besides, I had my gun, and they didn't have time to arm themselves."

"We're used to bears, wolves, and storms threatening our lives. But we've never really endured the worst threat of all."

"And what's that?"

"Other people. I always assume my family is safe here…"

"We *are* safe here."

"Not when Bill takes a pounding on his own porch, and my wife has to chase a pair of idiots away at gunpoint. You both could have been seriously hurt, Charlie."

"But we weren't… Well, except Bill. But his nose is as good as new now."

Oliver shook his head. "I'm tired of this. Bill has brought too much danger into our family."

"Bill is *part* of our family."

"No, love," Oliver got up and walked away from her, "he's not. He strolled into our lives out of the woods. We don't know a thing about him because he keeps his past to himself. We have no idea who we're dealing with! Remember Rick? He pulled a gun on us to get to Bill!"

"Rick hasn't bothered us in ages," Charlotte countered, although she knew she was fighting a losing battle.

"That's not the point. Where do you think those two muscle-heads came from? Rick obviously sent them."

"We don't know that—"

"Rick sent them," Bill interrupted, suddenly heading toward the couple.

Charlotte sighed. "Now's not the time, Bill."

"I needed to come and apologize to Oliver." Bill held his hat in front of him, his old, rough fingers nervously playing with the brim. "I put Charlotte in danger, and I'm very sorry. I don't know why Rick sent those guys here, but he obviously hasn't let the past go."

"I appreciate that, Bill. I really do. But that doesn't solve the problem. I can't sleep at night knowing some crazy guy out for revenge might wonder onto my property at any moment and endanger my family to get to you."

Bill nodded. "You're right, which is why I'll go into the city and sort things out. I just need time."

"Or," Oliver came in with a counter offer, "you could tell us what the heck is going on so that we know how to help you."

"I'm afraid I can't do that…"

Charlotte bit her lip. She knew Oliver didn't tolerate Bill's elusiveness as patiently as she did.

"That's not good enough for me anymore," Oliver said. "I want answers."

"I can't give them to you without…" Bill hesitated. His voice cracked. "I just can't, Olly."

Oliver scowled at the use of his pet name, which his mother and close family members had adopted. "Don't call me that," he grumbled, not considering his friendship with Bill to be on the same level. "And I'm sorry. You're might be important to my wife and kids, but as I've always told you, my priority is to keep my family safe."

Bill nodded slowly, the words clearly stinging.

A lump formed in Charlotte's throat. She couldn't bear watching two men she loved hurting each other. She rose quietly and tried to escape the conversation without notice.

"Charlie," Oliver called at her, "where are you going?"

"I can't handle this. I'm sorry," she managed before tears started flooding down her cheeks.

Oliver tried to draw her in for a hug, but she pulled herself free, pushing her way out of the door and stumbling down the steps as everything became a watery blur.

"Charlie!" Bill called after her.

Yet, she kept walking. She had work to do and an afternoon fishing trip to plan for their less-than-eager guests.

"You did this," Oliver hissed at Bill.

Charlotte had precisely five minutes of alone to sulk. She snuck into the restroom and seated herself on the closed lid of the toilet, sobbing as quietly as she could.

"Mommy," a little voice called from the other side of the door, "why are you crying?"

Charlotte sniffed. "Mommy's not crying. I'm fine, I promise."

"But I heard you and Daddy fighting," Amelia exclaimed.

"Mommy and Daddy had a loud talk, but we're fine."

"Then why are you hiding in here? You only come in here when you want to cry!"

"It's okay, Amelia," Charlotte soothed, trying to blow her clogged nose.

Amelia went silent for a moment before her own little sobs echoed over the toilet stall door.

"Amelia, love, why are *you* crying?"

She snuffled. "I'm not crying," she said defiantly.

Charlotte rolled her eyes, opened the door, and swept up her six-year-old into her arms. She gave her little girl a tight squeeze before talking to her. "Sometimes, Mommy and Daddy need some private time to talk about problems. And small people, like yourself, know they're not allowed to hide under the bed and listen to grown-up conversations."

Amelia's big eyes filled with tears again and she cried into her mother's shoulder. "I'm sorry, mommy. I want to be good, but it's just so hard!"

Charlotte tried to hide her smile as she carried her child out of the restroom and back to the little library where the children spent their morning with Rebekah doing lessons. "I found an escapee," she informed Rebekah with a wink, settling the sniffing Amelia down behind her desk.

"Sorry, Charlie. She snuck out during nap time," Rebekah explained.

"We're taking the new guests out fly-fishing late this afternoon. Oliver is going to teach Alf. I think Thomas can join. I believe Lola is interested in learning how to fish too, and I must keep Barb occupied, so I can't do it by myself."

Thomas buried his mortified face in his arms on his desk. "Take Benjamin," he instructed, his voice muffled. "I want nothing to do with Lola."

Charlotte and Rebekah exchanged a glance.

"Now, if I've taught you anything, young man," Rebekah scolded him, "it's that we always give each other second chances."

Thomas raised a pink face to scowl at her.

"Think of how many chances I've given you after you've escaped from my lessons day after day, Thomas Malik Bouchard!" she continued. "Don't you think Lola deserves another chance?"

"Fine," Thomas moaned. "I'll teach her how to fish, but I can tell you right now that her ugly face will scare all the fish away."

"Thomas!" a shocked Charlotte scolded. "We did *not* raise you to speak about other people like that, especially behind their backs!"

"I would tell her to her face, but I bet you wouldn't approve of that either!"

Charlotte stared in shock at her sweet son, who spent his days learning everything he could about nature, rescuing small creatures that were hurt, and teaching his little sister how to use the net to scoop up fish. Yet, suddenly, she stared at a typical, broody teenaged boy, nurturing a wounded heart.

"Sorry." He sighed. "I know that was rude. I don't know why I'm so angry, but that Lola girl just brings out the worst in me."

My darling boy is back, Charlotte thought in relief. But she wondered for how long.

Owen sniggered. "Love does that to a person."

And with that, sweet Thomas was gone again.

***

Charlotte watched as her husband gracefully showed how to flick the line back and forth before casting it into the waters.

Alf watched with a look of presumptuous ease, as though he didn't understand why he needed the demonstration in the first place.

Oliver drew his line back in and handed the rod to the overconfident politician who threw a smirk over his shoulder at his wife.

Barb was sitting at the bank on a picnic blanket watching the proceedings, while Charlotte busied herself making sure she'd brought everything they needed.

"Is everything all right between you and your husband?" Barb asked casually, wearing a knowing smile.

Charlotte bit back the urge to snarl and instead tried a more open approach. "Yeah," she said, laughing at herself. "I felt a little foolish telling you how wonderful my marriage is and then getting into a full-blown fight with my husband in front of you."

Barb seemed taken aback by Charlotte's humble response. "I have to admit, it was rather fun to see someone else losing it for a change. Though it helped me realize we need a drastic change in my family."

"All family's fight," Charlotte assured her.

"Yes. But I can tell that a fight in your family is a rare occasion, whereas it's the only way we know how to communicate in mine." Barb sighed.

"Was it always like that?" Charlotte asked timidly.

Barb shook her head. "No. That's the sad part. When Lola was born, Alf and I discovered a kind of blissful happiness that we'd never experienced before."

"What changed?"

"Alf started gaining popularity in the campaigns. Suddenly, we were living in the public eye. We had an image to maintain. I think over the years, all of our energy went into building the public image of the Columbus family, rather than developing a real, functioning family."

Charlotte gazed out at the fishing scene again, processing Barb's sad explanation. Alf had gotten his line tangled in some greenery growing near the lake. He tugged violently on the line while Oliver danced around, trying to stop Alf from snapping his rod in half.

"Alf's not a patient man anymore," Barb continued, watching the scene herself. "And he's paranoid. There have been a few incidents, and he doesn't trust anyone anymore. It's why I thought it best to travel out this way."

Distant giggles drifted over the surface of the lake and caught Charlotte's attention. She had almost forgotten that a reluctant Thomas was teaching an even less willing Lola how to fish. She wondered if the source of the giggling was from

Owen, who might have escaped Rebekah so he could build up ammunition for relentless teasing later.

But the giggling was from Lola. Thomas had been demonstrating a basic cast, his line sailing smoothly through the air. Lola had mimicked him perfectly, her own line floating a few meters ahead of her. The manic laughter had erupted when the pair had witnessed Alf hurling his rod with all his might into the depths of the lake and stomping in fury through the water, his waders slowing him down.

Charlotte watched with trepidation as Alf sloshed his way to shore, a peeved Oliver fighting to control his temper in the background while ducking into the freezing waters, trying to locate his fishing rod. She began hastily unpacking the picnic spread, careful not to leave any food unwrapped. The last thing they needed was a hungry bear to stumble upon their party.

"It's not that difficult," Lola teased her father from a distance.

Thomas grinned widely, suggesting that he and Lola had made peace and were working around each other's awkwardness.

"Mr. Columbus," Oliver said as the pair waded their way in, "I would appreciate it if next time you lose your temper, you might work hard not to lose my rod too."

"I'll buy you a new one," Mr. Columbus replied gruffly.

"You can't," Oliver snapped. "It was one of a kind."

"You don't get 'one of a kind' fishing rods," Alf Columbus countered, clearly unwilling to apologize.

"It *is* one of a kind to me. My father gave it to me."

"Well, I'll give him the money to buy you another one." Alf offered the condescending remark before downing half a glass of orange juice.

"You can't," Oliver remarked softly. "My father died on the mine. Besides, I found it, no thanks to you."

A deathly silence descended on the group. Alf, who was halfway through a sandwich, nearly choked. Barb began chastising her husband immediately, demanding he apologized to Oliver. Meanwhile, Lola and Thomas, who had also come in from the water, glared at each other.

"You don't have to apologize," Oliver broke the silence. "But I would prefer it if you treated my lodge, my gear, and my dear family with a little more respect while you're here."

Charlotte was gob-smacked. Her husband was typically the shy and reserved type, especially when important city folk arrived. He usually disappeared into the background, immersing himself in work while she dealt with the guests. Oliver almost never spoke up against guests, unless the situation was so severe that it demanded his attention.

Alf looked as though he was going to swing a punch. He exhaled slowly. Then, to everyone's surprise, Alf extended a pudgy hand in Oliver's direction. "There," he added hastily. "I apologize. Let's be gentlemen and shake on it."

Oliver gripped the man's hand and gave it a firm shake, maintaining respectful eye-contact.

Charlotte and Barb watched, amazed, as the two men chatted away over lunch as though nothing had happened, engaging each other in deep conversation about the different fish found in the lake. Soon, Thomas joined in, confidently adding titbits of his own knowledge, which Alf listened to attentively.

"I don't understand men," Lola commented to her mother. "One minute, they seem interested in you, and the next, they'd rather talk about fish."

Barb frowned, just as perplexed as her daughter.

The men waded out carefully into a good spot, and Barb watched as her husband beautifully casted a line, his fly drifting with the current until it was gulped down. The men worked in sync, Thomas and Oliver guiding Alf as he reeled in his catch.

"I think he's got something big," Charlotte said. "We must cook it up for dinner on a fire tonight."

"Cook a fish?" Lola asked, unable to keep the disgust from crinkling her upturned nose.

"You can eat it raw if you'd prefer," Charlotte said with a smile.

Lola was taken aback, unaccustomed to humor. But finally, she cracked a small smile, realizing Charlotte was joking. "I quite like sushi," she joked back shyly.

Celebratory sounds from the excited group of men drew the women's attention back to the lake. Alf was holding up a trout, its golden speckles shining in the light.

"Beautiful catch," Charlotte commented approvingly. "We must take a photo."

The family gathered around Alf, who held up the enormous fish with a wide grin on his face.

Charlotte was amazed by how much more attractive the family appeared when they weren't scowling, glaring, or sneering at each other. Lola laughed cheerfully, and even Barb cracked a sincere smile for the camera.

"I don't know how to thank you for this," Barb whispered to Charlotte while she was packing away the remnants of the picnic lunch.

"But I did nothing."

"This is the first time I've seen Alf smile, and I mean *really* smile, in more than a decade." Barb's eyes blurred with tears that she quickly wiped away with a practiced hand.

"I think it's the fresh air." Charlotte smiled. "It does wonders for a person."

"No, I think it's the fresh company. You're real, Charlotte Bouchard. You don't tip-toe around us because we're rich and famous, and neither does your husband. I feel like You treat us like real people, and we're able to relax and be ourselves for a change."

Charlotte felt her own eyes well with tears at Barb's words. "Thank you," she choked out.

"You have a beautiful family, Charlotte," Barb concluded.

"As do you." Charlotte winked.

Chapter 4
Ghostly Familiarities

Charlotte delivered the two cups of coffee to the porch. Bill and Oliver sat outside under the starry sky, discussing fishing and chatting away as if there was never a problem between them.

Charlotte agreed with Lola's observation; men were a difficult species to grasp.

Charlotte busied herself inside their cabin with stitching up the vast heap of torn clothes that had accumulated on her sewing table. As a mother of three and lodge an owner, she rarely had moments where she could sit down quietly and get the more mundane tasks done.

She pulled a shirt off the top of the pile and noticed it wasn't Oliver's. It smelled of Bill.

How quickly Bill had integrated himself into the family. Even his darning had been absorbed with theirs. Charlotte smiled as she threaded the needle and began patching up the tear.

A spot of blood on the collar of the shirt reminded her of the violent encounter the night before. She realized with horror that it was the same shirt Bill had been wearing when the two men had attacked. The tear she was sewing had been from the man who'd pulled Bill up.

A shudder went down Charlotte's spine and she cast the shirt aside, reaching for one of Oliver's instead. Words from the outdoor conversation drifted inside.

"I'm glad you could help them. That Alf seems like a tough character," Bill said.

"Oh boy, when he tossed my rod into the lake, I thought I was going to strangle him with my bare hands. I was so furious," Oliver admitted with a chuckle.

"Few men can hold their tempers when another man deals badly with their fishing gear, that's for sure." Bill laughed.

"I found the rod though," Oliver said. "I don't think I would have been as gracious had it been lost forever."

"Ah, the truth comes out." Bill grew serious. "I think you taught him something perhaps no one else ever took the time to."

Oliver raised an eyebrow. "What's that?"

"To respect other people. When certain people get to the top in life, they forget what it's like to be an ordinary human at the bottom. And they act as though they're superior to everyone else until someone like you comes along and reminds them we're all equal."

Charlotte couldn't hear Oliver's response. Knowing her husband, though, she figured he was pondering the significance of Bill's words.

"You're a good person, Olly," Bill continued, unperturbed by the silence. "You did the right thing. You always do the right thing."

She knew these words would irritate her husband. He hated being told that he was a good person because

Charlotte suspected that Oliver didn't believe this about himself.

"I'm no good person," he argued. "You don't know me well enough to understand that yet, Bill."

"I know you plenty well."

Oliver returned to the moment he'd almost lost his temper. "I think I would have attacked Alf, fancy politician or not, if that rod had been lost."

"Which rod did you take with you?"

"The red one," Oliver muttered, his voice barely audible.

"The one your father gave you," Bill said knowingly.

"What did you say?" Oliver asked sharply.

"The red rod. I've seen it in the boathouse. It's the one your father gave you…"

"How could you possibly know that?" Oliver's chair scraped on the floorboards.

Charlotte jumped as her needle pricked her finger. She'd been so engrossed in their conversation, she hadn't been paying attention to what her hands were doing.

Bill was silent for a moment. "You told me," he finally answered.

"No, I did not," Oliver said. "It's not a fact I share openly."

"Then it must have been Thomas or Benjamin. Everyone knows that rod is off limits." Bill tried to keep his voice casual.

"Yes, everyone knows the red rod is off limits, but very few people know my father gave it to me."

"Could you relax, Olly? You're putting me on edge. I'm telling you, I heard it somewhere."

"Olly…" Oliver muttered, repeating the pet name. "You keep calling me Olly."

"Sorry, I know that you don't like it."

The silence between them grew increasingly uncomfortable.

The tension seeped under the screen door and into the room Charlotte was working in. She stopped dabbing at the stain of blood she had left on Oliver's shirt and strained her ears to hear what was happening outside.

The two men were talking in angry but hushed whispers.

She set her sewing down and crept closer to the door, curiosity burning inside of her.

"No!" Oliver shouted angrily, causing Charlotte to jump a foot as he crashed through the screen door.

"Olly, love," Charlotte said, following him to their bedroom, "what's wrong?"

Oliver pulled a bag out from under their bed, fury pulsating off him. As he threw clothes into the bag, his hands shook.

"What's going on?" Charlotte asked, eyeing the camping gear he placed on top of his clothes.

"I need to get away from here," he finally answered through gritted teeth.

"*What*?" Charlotte blinked in disbelief. "You can't just leave! Talk to me!"

"This is too big," Oliver exploded. "I'm sorry, I just can't be here. I can't breathe here. I need space."

Angry tears streaked his face. So furious, he couldn't even meet Charlotte's eye. He zipped his bag and slung it over his shoulder. He then exited the room and pulled out a tent along with a couple other items, before kicking his way through the screen door. Before leaving the porch, he turned and gave her a hasty kiss on the lips.

"Charlie, I love you with all my heart, but I just need to get away and process things. This has nothing to do with you," he explained, his cheeks still wet with tears. "Talk to Bill if you want answers." With that, he disappeared into the darkness.

Charlotte's mind imploded with a million questions. She knew her husband well enough to know he was going camping to clear his mind for a day or two, and then he'd be back. Being in nature was where he found his peace. Still, it broke her heart when he disappeared without explanation.

"Mommy," Amelia's voice found her for the second time that day, "where's daddy going?"

"He's taking a brief holiday." Charlotte forced a smile.

"Why does he never take us with him?" Owen asked.

"Because he needs some quiet time to think," Thomas answered, understanding his father. He could answer for him, because he was most like him with being in the great outdoors.

"Do you want to go with him, Tom?" Charlotte asked her son.

"No. I think Dad needs this one alone," he answered wisely.

"Right. Let's all get back into bed. Daddy loves you very much. He thought you were sleeping. Otherwise, he would have given you all kisses before going."

While she read a good night story, tucked each child back into bed, and delivered three extra rounds of goodnight kisses, Charlotte's mind replayed snatches of the conversation she'd overheard, trying to make sense of what had her husband so upset.

"Mommy, what's wrong?" Amelia asked in a sleepy voice, her eyes barely open.

"Nothing, love. Mommy is just thinking about why Daddy left, that's all."

"Okay." Amelia smiled at her. "Is it because Uncle Bill is actually Daddy's daddy?"

Charlotte stared at her six-year-old. "Why would you say that?"

"Thomas told me," she answered with a yawn before her eyes closed again.

Charlotte cast a glance at Thomas, who'd miraculously fallen fast asleep.

Chapter 5
More Packed Bags

"Would you care to explain what's going on?" Charlotte demanded, kicking open Bill's door.

"It's considered polite to knock, you know?"

"Are you Oliver's father?"

He answered Charlotte's vicious question with silence.

"What the hell, Bill? Or should I say *Malik*?" Charlotte paced his living room, her hands lost in her tangled hair.

"I'm sorry, Charlie," Bill muttered under his breath. "You would never understand."

"That's not fair! You didn't even give me the chance to understand! How does my fourteen-year-old son know that you're Grandpa Malik and I'm left in the dark?!"

"He figured it out," Bill grumbled. "I didn't tell him."

"How?" she demanded again, her voice raising another uncomfortable crescendo.

"Thomas doesn't just look with his eyes. He looks with his heart."

This silenced Charlotte's fuming. It was four in the morning. She had laid awake all night, tossing and turning until she'd finally given up on sleep and went to confront Bill, fearing he might disappear at first light. "I want the truth," she demanded.

"I'm Malik Bouchard."

Charlotte's voice caught in her throat. Wiping away tears, she refocused on Bill. "But Malik Bouchard died at the mine."

"He did. Malik's identity died, and then Bill was born."

"You had a family that adored you. Why disappear? I don't get it! This isn't some kind of spy thriller movie."

"I had a family that didn't know me anymore. They didn't need me. The letters slowly faded as time passed. I knew what they really needed most…"

"What? What could they have possibly needed more than you?"

"Money. Olivia had written to say she'd bought this piece of land and planned out a lodge. But it would have taken fifty years to build. With my pathetic cheque, she never would have been able to afford this."

"Oliver and his mother didn't start the lodge for money. They began things here out of boredom from waiting for you."

"What do you mean?"

"Olivia wanted to return to her family, but Oliver refused. He wanted to wait for you. He feared that if they left, you would never come home. Then he met me and fell in love. And of course, the only home I've ever known is Canada. I came from Fond du Lac. So that cemented Oliver's desire to stay in Saskatchewan and turn it into a home. His mother came up with the lodge idea, and so they slowly built it. Oliver never gave up waiting for you." Charlotte's voice broke. "Until the day the letter arrived."

Charlotte remembered the day clearly as she related it to Bill. She had been painting sealant on the front porch of the lodge. His mother was cooking fish on an outdoor fire for lunch. In the background sat three little humble tents they'd been living in until Oliver put on the roof. Oliver had been hewing a tree trunk into workable pieces so he could begin building his first guest cabin.

A Mounty arrived on a horse. His grave face and stiff manner alerted Olivia that something was very wrong. Holding a letter in his shaking fingers, he extended a red-jacketed arm. Olivia immediately knew the contents and refused to take it.

In desperation, the Mounty turned his outstretched hand to a puzzled Oliver, who accepted the letter. Charlotte had watched as he ripped the envelop open and unfolded the short sheet of condolence from the mine in Uranium City. The last fold of the letter revealed a cheque of considerable fortune.

"It was a payout for the 'accidental death of Malik Bouchard,'" Charlotte quoted. "Oliver dropped the letter and cheque in the dirt, packed up his tent and fishing gear, and disappeared into the woods for a month. But he returned once he had grieved and coped with the anguish of knowing you would never come home." Charlotte fixed Bill with a pointed stare.

"Well," Bill stated defensively, "it's thanks to that cheque that you and Oliver have all of this." He gestured to the surrounding lodge.

Charlotte shook her head. "No," she muttered, her breath catching in her chest again. "Oliver refused to spend a dime. He called it blood money and wanted nothing to do with it."

"*What*? I paid a high price for that payout, and he didn't even use it?"

"Clearly," Charlotte threw back. "Did you cut a deal with Rick? Is that where he fits into all this?"

Bill averted his gaze at the sound of Rick's name.

"So, he had something to do with your mysterious disappearance all those years ago," Charlotte concluded.

Bill slumped into a chair. His face paled at the dread of having to face the past.

"No more lies, Bill," Charlotte said.

"Fine." He wiped his face with his hand. "Rick approached me. I think he has a gift for smelling out desperate men. He knew everything about my family, my financial status, and the years I had left to work on my contract. He started whispering in my ear about a way to make a lot of money so that my family would never have to worry again."

"What did you have to do?"

"I had to follow Rick's instructions. And those instructions were on how to fake my death and implicate the mine." Shame filled Bill's lined face. "I had no idea Rick was doing this with several others too. I couldn't have known he used that slow process to take down the mine until one day, its doors were shut permanently and thousands lost their jobs."

Charlotte shook her head. She thought of Uranium City—a once thriving place bustling with economic growth and promise that had been rendered a ghost town with two hundred residents.

"I know you must hate me," Bill croaked. "And I don't blame you in the slightest. I hate myself."

"Bill," Charlotte whispered, "I mean Malik…" The name was unfamiliar on her tongue, "how could I hate you?"

He cried into his hands, decades of pent-up emotions flooding through. "I ruined so many people's lives."

"I can't imagine what you've endured keeping this inside of you," Charlotte said. "It must have eaten you up every day. How could you stand to be around us, knowing who we were?"

"Part of the deal with Rick was that once Oliver and my wife received the cheque, I would disappear. If the mine ever caught wind that I was still alive, it would mean *a lot* of trouble. So, I vanished. But…" he hesitated again, his throat dry as he choked back the pain, "I couldn't keep away. I had to see you all."

"Why didn't you just tell us?" Charlotte pleaded. "We would have understood."

"That was never part of the plan. I was just supposed to see you from a distance. And then I would disappear again, comforted by the knowledge that it had all been worth it and my Oliver could enjoy a happy life with his family, surrounded by wealth and prosperity."

Charlotte shook her head. "What he really longed for was a father."

"I didn't know that I would stumble across him fishing that day in the woods. I recognized him immediately, but knew he would never know who I was after all the decades I'd been in the mine. But then the bear arrived, and he was set on having Oliver for lunch." He chuckled through his tears. "I knew I couldn't disappear. I had to save my son."

Charlotte remembered that day. She'd ridden out to find Oliver, realizing something was wrong when his horse returned without him.

"Oliver insisted I return with him. I could hardly speak. He said he would give me work and a place to stay, and I figured I would just sneak away in the night, but then…"

"What?"

"Then I saw you." He smiled. "Riding up on your horse, your hair flowing in the wind… I knew I could never leave again."

"Why?" Charlotte asked, confused. "You'd never even met me."

"You gave me hope that my wife might still wait for me at your lodge. I didn't know Olivia was gone. But you—you were so kind, Charlie. So non-judgmental. You took me in, cleaned me up, and set me right in life."

"I knew there was a reason you felt like instant family."

"I don't know how Thomas figured it out." Bill shook his head. "Thomas must have had a lot of old photos because one day, he handed me a picture of myself. He didn't say a word. He just sat there fishing in silence, perfectly content to know that he had a grandfather. I promised myself that I would tell you and Oliver, but I just couldn't."

"So instead, you grew your horrible beard back in case anyone else went through the old photo albums?"

"I'm sorry for the pain I have caused you, Charlie."

"You've brought a kind of joy to our lives we didn't know we were missing." Charlotte got up from her chair and dropped to her knees in front of Bill. "Please, don't do what I know you're planning to."

His eyes flicked inevitably to the half-packed satchel on his bed. "I have to," he said in a hoarse whisper. "I've caused so much damage."

"So, don't cause anymore! Stop disappearing! It'll break our hearts."

"Oliver has told me to go on over one occasion, and he's right. As long as I'm anywhere near you, Rick won't stop. I'm a threat to him."

"Then go to Corporal Dumont and tell him the truth," Charlotte suggested, her fingers clinging to Bill's arm. "He's a fair agent of the law, and he likes you."

"And then what? Spend the rest of my life in prison?" Bill pushed her away. "No. If I go, then Rick will leave you alone. It's what Oliver wants. It's what I want."

"You're family, Malik and not just a father now. You're a grandfather too, and there are three little kids who will be devastated if you leave them."

"Not to Oliver. In his eyes, I died a long time ago. I knew the minute he figured things out, he would have preferred I had stayed dead."

"That's not true! Oliver just needs time to work through this. I promise, he'll come back, wanting to talk things through with you."

Bill shook his head. "I'm sorry, Charlie. This is goodbye." He stooped to kiss the top of her head.

"Please," Charlotte begged, burying her face in her hands. "I can't carry this alone."

The screen door banged with a loud thud, and Charlotte realized Bill was already gone.

Chapter 6
The Empty Nest

The remainder of the day passed Charlotte in a blur.

Alf Columbus had become obsessed with his new passion for fishing and was determined to change his wife's abhorrence of the slippery, armored, cold-blooded creatures. Disappointed that Oliver was unavailable to mentor him, Alf had settled with being taken out for the day by Benjamin, the head fishing guide.

Charlotte placed Madison in charge of overseeing the running of the lodge for the day. And since this upset a jealous Rebekah to the point of rioting, Charlotte conjured a plan to remove the problem. Feeling equally ill-equipped to deal with four children, Charlotte sent them out fishing for the morning. Rebekah, along with a second fishing guide, accompanied the children under the guise of warding off hungry bears, while really, Charlotte just needed some precious alone time.

To keep her mind off things, Charlotte secluded herself in their small greenhouse and dug away heatedly in the vegetable patch. She savagely attacked the weeds and ripped out anything she couldn't verify as edible.

Chef Victor ran out furiously, his arms flailing wildly, and dragged her away from a heap of shredded leafy greens when he realized she'd been hacking at his potato plants. "What's gotten into you?" he demanded, his dark eyes ablaze as they scanned over the carnage.

Charlotte dissolved into a heap on the ground, her face streaked with dirt, sweat, and tears.

Victor mumbled something about 'woman hormones' before helping her up and hauling her to the kitchen, where he forced her to eat an entire meal and a slice of chocolate cake.

Afterwards, Charlotte had to admit, she felt a trifle better. She realized with everything that had happened, her last meal had been the day before. Victor then called in Madison and gave her strict orders to make sure Charlotte went to bed and got some rest.

Exhausted, Charlotte's final thoughts were of her husband and Bill before she lost all consciousness.

"Charlie," a voice disturbed her dreams.

With great effort, she dragged her numb mind back to the land of the living and forced herself to accept the awful memories of her current reality. She checked her watch with one eye barely open. "How long have I been asleep?"

"A couple of hours."

"Did you drug me?" Charlotte asked in a croaky voice as she tried to sit up. The room started spinning.

"That's not important right now," Madison said. "How long was Rebekah supposed to be out with the kids?"

"If you're trying to get her into trouble—"

"I'm not, I promise. It's just, I thought they were coming back for lunch at the lodge."

"That was the plan," Charlotte affirmed.

"Well, they're two hours late."

"What?" Charlotte's eyes widened with alarm. "Being late isn't allowed!"

Her children and staff knew better than to lose track of time when out on an excursion; it was one of their strict policies. Everyone wore a watch, and everyone stuck rigidly to the clock. It was a safety precaution in a time where the radio was the only form of communication available, and even so, the lodge didn't possess portable radios. Running late meant there was a problem.

Two hours late equated to an emergency.

"Get my rifle," Charlotte ordered, swinging her feet out of bed and into her boots.

"I can go," Madison suggested. "You need some rest."

"No," Charlotte dismissed her suggestion. "And it's not because I don't think you can take on a bear—which I don't. It's just that I need you here running the lodge. We're a little understaffed."

"You can't go alone! Not with everything going through your mind!"

"I know," Charlotte conceded, buttoning her shirt and grabbing a rain jacket and a flashlight. "I'll take a guide with me."

"Nick is still around, if you'd prefer him. He's more used to a horse than some of the guides."

"Call Nick. We leave in two minutes," Charlotte announced, swinging her backpack and rifle over her shoulder.

The two minutes it took Nick to reach her at the stable felt like an hour. Charlotte was in the process of beating herself up for not keeping it together. She was the mother. Mothers weren't allowed days where they suffered mental and emotional breakdowns and sent their kids off into the woods. It didn't matter if every man she'd ever relied on walked out on her within twelve hours of each other. She was supposed to keep it together.

"What's on your mind, Charlie?" Nick asked, knowing her well enough to read the signs of troubled thoughts.

They listened to the horses' hooves clatter along the well-worn path while Charlotte fought to overcome her pride and express herself to the young pilot.

"I hope they haven't done something stupid, Nick." Charlotte shook her head as she kicked her horse into a faster pace, primarily to hide her crumbling façade of strength.

"Is this the speed we're going to go at?" Nick asked as his horse bolted forward to keep up.

Charlotte glowered at him. "I know the spot they were fishing from. Once we're there, we can slow down and look for signs," she explained, her voice husky and her eyes wet with emotion.

"Look, Charlie, I know they're your kids and all, but I'm sure they're fine. They probably just lost track of time."

"Have you met my kids?" Charlotte said sarcastically. "Oliver went on one of his 'alone time' camping trips and then Bill abandoned camp this morning. By now, my kids have not only figured this out, but they have also decided it is within their power to fix things."

"So you think your three kids, along with the snotty guest kid, are on a mission to track down Oliver and Bill and bring them back?"

Charlotte slowed briefly while she reconsidered her theory. "You're right. It is pretty ridiculous. Sorry, I'm just paranoid. You know what Thomas is like when he's dealing with something like this."

Nick laughed without humor. "I hate to say it, but I don't think you're being paranoid. I can imagine your kids doing something like that."

Charlotte rolled her eyes and forced herself to take in a deep breath so that she wouldn't verbally attack him. "You know what would really help?"

"What?"

"You keeping quiet."

Nick directed a surly scowl at her, but nodded. "Sorry. I know I turn everything into a joke." He offered her a small reassuring smile.

"That's because you don't have the maturity levels to deal with serious life situations," Charlotte fussed.

"Ouch." Nick clutched his heart, mocking offense.

Charlotte winked.

The two of them then maintained a steady pace until the clearing at the edge of the lake loomed into view and Charlotte knew they'd reached the right spot.

"Sounds quiet," Nick said, swinging his leg over the back of his horse and landing with a thump on the ground.

"*Too* quiet," Charlotte agreed, drawing her rifle.

The pair carefully moved forward, their feet instinctively avoiding dry leaves and twigs.

Charlotte noticed the abandoned fishing rods lying carelessly in the dirt. "This isn't like them at all," she muttered. The picnic basket had been overturned. She crouched over and identified the fox spoor, which explained why the basket was devoid of all its food content. "Also not like them not to devour the contents of their picnic basket within the first five minutes."

"There's no one here," Nick stated the obvious, his boyish face confused.

"Looks like there was a scuffle of sorts over here. It couldn't have been the kids wrestling because there are adult prints as well."

"Rebekah?" Nick shouted into the trees around them. Birds scurried into flight and squirrels zigzagged the ground in a hurry to get away.

Charlotte gave Nick a disapproving look.

He ignored her. "Your kids are smart, but they couldn't have gotten away from two adults that easily."

Charlotte raised her eyebrows and prayed Nick's underestimation of her children was somehow correct.

"Wait," he muttered, the dread evident in his voice.

Charlotte followed his line of sight and charged forward. "Rebekah? Oh my goodness…" She dropped to her knees at Rebekah's side.

The tutor had been gagged and tied to a tree. She had a nasty gash on her head, and looked as though she was unconscious.

"Here's Pete," Nick shouted, referring to the fishing guide who'd accompanied the kids.

Charlotte worked furiously at the tight knots until Rebekah's blue hands and feet were finally free.

"Charlie?" she croaked in an uncertain voice. "Ow, my head…" Her dirty fingers traced the dried blood at the source of the wound.

"You're okay, Beca," Charlotte assured her.

"Pete is alive," Nick announced, relieved.

"Rebekah," Charlotte forced the dazed tutor to focus, "I need to know what happened."

"The kids…"

"They're gone, Beca. Where are they?"

Rebekah shook her head, tears blurring her eyes. "I'm so sorry," she whispered, her entire frame trembling.

"Tell me what happened," Charlotte demanded, working hard to remain patient.

"Two men," Rebekah managed through quivering lips. "They came. They took them."

"We tried to stop them, Charlie," Pete's emotionally wrought voice pierced her ears, "but they had guns."

Charlotte's eyes snapped back to Rebekah's lips as they formed the words, "They're gone. I'm so sorry."

Thomas felt the rough hessian sack being roughly pulled off his head. He was blinded by early afternoon sunlight. Instinctively, he twisted his head, scanning the waters around him for a familiar island, rock, or tree. But he couldn't identify anything. "Let me go!" he demanded bravely.

"Shut up, kid," a gruff voice commanded.

Thomas was slapped hard on the back of his head. He bit away the pain, his vision slightly blurred from the rough hit.

"I told you to be gentle with them!" the second man complained. "They're just kids. We're no kid-killers!"

"Speak for yourself, Denver," the harsher voice argued. "I would be perfectly happy to knock off one or two of these kids if I get pushed any further. The small one bit me. She actually *bit* me!"

Thomas grinned at the memory of the men trying to grab them. Amelia had put her new set of teeth to good use, biting down on any hands, fingers, and even a nose that came within range.

Owen had screamed for an hour, no gag was thick or tight enough to stop his shrieking, although Denver had refused to allow any permanent harm to come to him.

Lola was well-trained when it came to self-defense as a young woman growing up in the city. She had a rather unique skill set, which she'd used effectively on Denver once and Louis twice. Louis was still walking with a limp, and he threatened that if he had been rendered permanently infertile, he was going to end her life.

Thomas, the oldest in the group, had remained calm. Robbed of his sight, he'd used his senses to try tracking where they were going. He knew the point at which they'd boarded a boat. He even knew the direction they had travelled in for some time. But once Louis realized what he was doing, he'd taken the boat around in several circles and detoured, trying to confuse Thomas.

Sadly, it had worked.

Thomas had been sitting with his hands tied behind his back, leaning against Lola, who was in a similar position. He suddenly felt her fingers worm into his.

"I'm scared, Tom," she whispered.

"We'll be okay," he assured her.

"Ooh," Owen crooned, witnessing the entire scene. "Tom's in love!"

"I swear, if you don't shut up, I'll toss you in the lake and watch the fish eat you!" Louis roared at an impervious Owen.

"I can swim with my hands tied behind my back," Owen said, unperturbed.

"Owen," Thomas cautioned, "stop. We need to start listening, okay? It's what Mom and Dad would want us to do."

Owen nodded, a grin briefly appearing on his face at the mention of their beloved parents. Shortly thereafter, however the grin was replaced with a look of tragic sorrow and he started to weep, quietly at first, but quickly gaining momentum. When Amelia heard her older brother crying, she followed suit, and soon, the tranquil lapping of the water against the shoreline was drowned out by the increasing crescendo of depressing wails and howls.

Chapter 7
Ransom

"What do you mean, 'Lola was with them'?" Alf exploded.

"All the kids are missing," Charlotte repeated as calmly as she could. In reality, her brain was disorientated, and she wasn't sure she was even forming coherent words. The faux calm she displayed was likely a byproduct of the adrenaline coursing through her entire being.

Charlotte took a shaky breath and continued. "Rebekah and Pete explained that two armed men ambushed them while they were unpacking."

"Not our Lola," Barb's voice trembled. "This can't be happening! We're supposed to be *safe* here. We chose this place so that nothing like this could happen again."

Charlotte watched as the shaking, gasping, frail woman fainted on the carpet.

Alf wasted several second contemplating whether he should assist his fallen wife, or take advantage of the silence.

"Alf," Charlotte scolded him, realizing he had selected the latter.

"I was going to help her," he said defensively, springing into embarrassed action.

Charlotte raised an eyebrow at him but decided against chastising the man when he was already facing a dire situation.

"What do you mean you were supposed to be safe here?" Charlotte asked, repeating Barb's last words.

Alf rubbed his forehead. "Not everyone is happy about me gaining power in the political world. I took quite an aggressive stance against some of our problems in the community, and it wasn't well received by everyone," he explained diplomatically, using his political tongue.

"Give it to me in simple terms," Charlotte said, aware of his tricks.

The large man sighed, a wave of sorrow passing over his face. "There was an attempted kidnapping before. Someone tried to grab Lola after school. Fortunately, a teacher nearby saw and put up a fight. But ever since then, we've been brutally aware of the fact that people can hurt us in the worst way possible, so we have to take extra precautions."

Charlotte paced, her footsteps muffled by the thick Persian rug covering the wooden floor. "But if your family is always in the public eye, the kidnappers would know to take Lola, and only Lola," Charlotte intoned, struggling to collect the thoughts from her scrambled brain.

Alf frowned. "I don't follow."

"Why take on the burden of three extra children? Especially three extra extremely loud, stubborn, and difficult children who would have put up a fight. I saw Owen get into a fight with a squirrel over his sandwich. My kids don't back down. You would need *a lot* of hands to manage my bunch."

"Perhaps your children could help identify the kidnappers, and that's why they took them too," Alf countered, though he was seeing Charlotte's point. "We sent Lola on a self-defense course after the incident, but she still would have cried. I'm glad that she's not alone, even though that means your children are also in danger. I'm sorry."

Charlotte dismissed his insensitivity as a reaction to the situation. If she was honest, though, she was more hopeful about getting their kids back since Thomas was in the group. "But they left Pete and Rebekah alive. They could have just tied up my kids too, but they didn't."

"What are you suggesting?" Alf asked, suddenly aware that Charlotte was hiding information of her own.

Charlotte inhaled deeply and studied the severity of Alf's mood before deciding whether to continue. She summoned what little courage she had and proceeded. "A couple of nights ago, before your family arrived, we may have had a slight incident on the property... Two men snuck in and tried to attack one of our staff members. Bill. They had bad dealings with each other in the past. Bill has since left, and I suspect those two idiots may have returned to find him."

"So you think they stole our children to get at this Bill character?" Alf's said, spittle flying from his lips. His face turned a concerning shade of purple and his eyes bulged.

Barb, who had revived, scolded her husband. "Sit down before you drop dead from a heart attack!"

"Can everyone just calm down, please?" Charlotte plead for the hundredth time that afternoon.

"Where is Oliver?" Alf asked. "You need a man to take charge in situations like this."

"You're the political *leader*," his wife taunted. "Why don't you take charge?"

"Because I'm not the one with a blasted gun license!"

"Oliver isn't here," Charlotte said, her voice threatening to break as she realized how utterly defeated she felt. "All you've got is me, okay? There's no one else."

"Can't you get the police out here to start a search?" Alf insisted.

Charlotte gulped; she'd been dreading this question. "You see, the cloud cover outside? That means we have no radio signal. Madison has been trying to reach the corporal for the last hour without success. We'll only be able to alert the Mounties to our situation when the weather clears."

Alf fell backwards into his chair, his face pale. Barb, who had made the foolish decision to try to stand up, flopped back down on the carpet, unconscious again.

"You mean to tell me we have no idea who took our children, and we have no way of getting help to find them?" Alf said, his booming voice shaking the picture frames on the wall.

"Charlie?" Madison's urgent voice rescued her from having to answer.

"Please tell me you reached the corporal?" Charlotte said.

Madison shook her head. "I'm afraid not, but we received a transmission of sorts."

"From who?"

Madison's fingers fidgeted with a small piece of paper in her hands. "It's not good."

"What does it say?" Charlotte demanded, snatching the note.

It read: *You have what I want, and I have what you want. Give me our old mutual friend, or I'll start depositing little ones at the bottom of the lake.*
Your friend from the city.

"Charlie," Madison stammered, "who would write all this nonsense? Who's your friend from the city, and who's the 'mutual friend'?"

Charlotte sighed. "Rick Neilson. He's behind all of this. And it must stop. He's saying if I don't hand over Bill, he'll start killing off the kids."

Madison's face paled.

Charlotte crumpled the note and tossed it at Alf. "The kidnapper made contact," she informed him.

He scanned the note in complete bewilderment, his face a wash of confusion. "Where are you going?" Alf yelled at Charlotte as he struggled to free himself from the sofa. He stepped over his wife lying on the carpet to scuttle after Charlotte.

"I'm going to get our children back," Charlotte declared.

"Well, I'm coming with you."

Charlotte didn't have the heart to refuse him. Nor did she have the right. He was a parent just the same as her, and his desire to save his daughter equaled her own.

"There's someone I need to find first," Charlotte said. "But I promise, I'll come back for you. I just need you to trust me and wait for my return."

Alf stared at her, eyes blazing for a moment before finally yielding with a humble nod.

Chapter 8
Counter Attack

Charlotte was more familiar with Uranium City the second time she visited. It had been a bumpy plane ride, but Nick had risen to the challenge, whirring the little aluminum frame through the turbulence as though it were a jet. Charlotte hurled her lunch into a bush the moment they landed.

"Sorry," Nick said. "Although, I think it's because you're upset about the kids."

"No," Charlotte said, rinsing her mouth with a glug of water. "It's definitely your flying. It's always your flying."

Nick scowled at her, but remembered they didn't have time to waste arguing.

"We've got about three hours before we have to make the flight back. Otherwise, we'll be out of daylight and I can feel a rather nasty storm brewing."

Charlotte nodded, feeling the electric tinge in the air as well. The storm would likely break over the lake rather than make it to where they were on the shore, but it was ludicrous to bet on the unpredictable northern Canadian weather.

"Do you think Bill would have really come back here?" Nick asked, his eyebrows crossed dubiously.

"Yeah, Bill doesn't have anywhere else to go. I think I know where to find him," Charlotte stated sadly.

Nick checked his watch. "I'll meet you back at the plane in three hours then."

Charlotte did the same, gave him a final nod, and kicked into a light jog towards the center of town.

Charlotte kicked open the termite-eaten door of the now familiar dingy bar. It was the second time she had ventured inside. The previous occasion had been to glean information about Bill's past with Rick, and it hadn't ended well, considering Rick had found and threatened her.

Those threats clearly hadn't been empty.

Charlotte was growing tired of Rick's ominous presence in her small world. She almost prayed she had the chance to run into him again. This time, she would be the one making the threats.

She scanned the odious room that reeked of sour beer, rancid peanuts, and bad breath, all the while ignoring the bleary-eyed faces grinning her way. "Where's Bill?" she asked in a loud voice that silenced the jeering.

"Why, hello little lady," the bartender said. "Aren't you going to order a drink first?"

"The last time I accepted help from you, you sold me out to Rick Neilson," she fired at him, pairing her words with an equally scathing stare.

The bartender's bushy eyebrows joined at the center in a contemptuous scowl. "Everyone in here needs to play by the rules, so don't come and—"

"Bill!" Charlotte suddenly roared over the bartender's voice. "I know you're hiding somewhere in here among these dirty scumbags, and I don't have time to play games, so come out!" She waited, ignoring the awkward silence and gawking eyes that slowly processed her insult.

"He's not here, sweety," a raspy voice informed her. "Although, us 'dirty scumbags' might not know for sure."

"Sorry about that," a red-faced Charlotte said. "Does anyone know where he is?" She cleared her throat before adding a timid, "Please?"

Yet, despite the added politeness, her question was ignored. The men returned to nurturing their drinks and sharing crude jokes.

"Look, I know I was rude and I'm sorry," Charlotte said. "I assumed the worst about all of you, and that wasn't fair."

They continued ignoring her, some even talking louder, so she had to shout to make herself heard.

"Have any of you ever been wronged by Rick Neilson?" she asked in desperation.

A few curious stares flickered her way.

"Rick has just taken everything from me," she continued, her voice cracking. "I know some of you here must know what that feels like."

A few more heads angled her way.

"He forced Bill, my father-in-law, to go on the run. Then he sent two of his thugs to kidnap my children."

This last sentence demanded the undivided attention of all in the bar, and some knowing eyes softened as though understanding the pain in her voice.

"Rick Neilson has threatened to kill my children if I don't give him what he wants," Charlotte said, ignoring the hot tears running down her cheeks.

"So, you're going to give him Bill?" a voice demanded. "He's one of us!"

"No," Charlotte snapped. "Of course not! But I need Bill's help to take down Rick. Now, I know some of you must be on Rick's side, but if there are any of you who've been wronged by Rick, then take this opportunity to stand on the side of justice and tell me where Bill is. I beg of you."

"He's right behind you, honey," the same raspy voice informed her.

Charlotte dropped her head to her chest and bit down the hundred remarks about how this was not the time for jokes.

"No, really, he's standing behind you," the voice insisted.

Charlotte felt a familiar hand weigh down on her shoulder. She spun round. "Bill!" she gasped. "I mean, *Malik*," she corrected herself before bounding into his chest and hugging him.

"I was about to take my one ticket out of here when the old woman on the corner mentioned you were in town."

"We need to go," Charlotte said, pulling him to the door he had just entered from. "Thank you!" she yelled over her shoulder to the bar, which was now cheering and chanting her name.

"If you came all of this way to convince me to come back with you, you're wasting your time," Malik said.

"He took the kids! Not just ours, but the politician's kid too."

"And you're sure Rick was behind it?"

Charlotte leveled a stare at him.

"All right, I get it. Who else would do such a thing?"

"He contacted Madi over the radio and left his demands. He wants you delivered to him, or he kills the kids. You know him better than I do. Would Rick really go to such lengths?"

Malik nodded grimly while scratching his gray beard. "He likely hasn't attached himself to the crime in any easily detectable way, so yes, he has no qualms about getting rid of a few kids."

Charlotte's bottom lip , and she bit down on it to steady herself. There was no way they could even link the ransom letter to him.

"Don't worry," Bill said with a resigned sigh. "I'll hand myself in."

"Oh no, you won't," Charlotte objected. "I refuse to lose you again, not after just finding out I have you. I have a better plan."

Malik frowned.

"Rick took something from me," Charlotte continued, "so to level the playing field, I'll take something from him."

"But he doesn't have any children or known family."

"I will not kidnap anybody," she retorted, her expression one of horror as she wondered at Bill's moral compass. "But there has to be something we could take to give us the upper hand. Money, jewelry, documents…"

They thought in silence, Charlotte hoping Malik would have a suggestion.

"I know just the thing." He suddenly snapped his fingers, a spark entering his old eyes.

"What is it?"

"A book." Malik grinned. "I can't believe I didn't think of this blackmail years ago."

"Blackmail? Look, Malik, I'm still an upstanding citizen of the law. If it weren't for Corporal Dumont being off in the middle of the woods somewhere, I would be at his front door right now."

Malik waved her concerns aside. "Relax. I've only seen it twice, but Rick keeps a little black book. Literally."

"How would that help us?"

"Well, as far as I can work out, a man trying to function at the level of dishonesty that Rick does needs to have some kind of record of who he's hired, who's doing what, and proof of his payments and transactions."

Charlotte shook her head in disbelief. "Nobody would be stupid enough to keep all of that in a book."

"This is real life. Criminal masterminds aren't like in the movies. They forget stuff. And forgetting stuff in the world of crime can end you up in jail."

"So can a record of all your past crimes collected in a single book."

"Exactly. If we get our hands on that book, Rick will explode. His life out of jail is more important to him than his old fight with me," Malik assured.

"How do we get it? Surely he would keep something like that on him."

"Not a chance. If he ever got into the hands of a Mounty, he would carry with him all the evidence needed to put him away for a very long time."

Charlotte checked the height of the sun in the sky and gauged how much daylight they had left. "Well, we've got less than two hours. So what do we do?"

"Rick has a hideout on the edge of town," Malik explained, his brow furrowed. "Few people know about it. And of course, he would have guards there."

Charlotte bit her lip and nervously ran her fingers through her hair. Her stomach twisted at the prospect of breaking into a criminal typhoon's home and robbing him. She shook her head as she mentally backed out of her ambitious plan. Then she thought of Thomas—brave and fearless—but in no way prepared to deal with the likes of Rick and his armed thugs. She thought of little Owen and Amelia, their permanent smiles and childhood innocence snatched from them.

"Okay, I'm ready," Charlotte declared, more for herself than for Malik.

"Follow me," Malik said, a mysterious look shadowing his old face.

***

Nick had been waiting at his plane for close on three hours without a glimpse of Charlotte. They were running out of time. He had already searched the center of town, but Charlotte was nowhere in sight.

Nick anxiously chewed his thumbnail and checked his watch for the hundredth time before a voice broke through his thoughts.

"Start the plane!" Charlotte yelled as soon as she was in sight.

Nick jumped. Charlotte was hurtling towards him from across the grassy field as fast as her strong little legs could carry her.

"What the heck?" Nick mumbled, watching openmouthed as Charlotte waved frantically at him from a distance. As a red-cheeked Charlotte loomed closer, Nick noticed a slower figure running behind her. "Bill?" he muttered, even more confused.

"Nick!" Charlotte screamed, her voice hoarse. "Start your stupid plane!"

Nick watched for a second longer and saw a third, enormous figure staggering his way over the top of the hill. A glimpse of the man's angry, purple face was enough to convince Nick that trouble was heading their way, and he needed to get his plane in the air, fast.

"What are you waiting for?" an out of breath Charlotte screamed. "Get in the plane!"

Nick hopped in the pilot's seat and started the engine. He had to wait for the oil temperature to climb before they could safely take off. Glancing out of the window, he judged that Charlotte would be there within a few seconds, followed by Bill. But he wasn't sure if they'd have an extra guest abroad or not.

The purple-faced man was cursing them. Behind him, a second security guard type ranged into view.

"What the hell did you do, Charlie?" Nick growled over the roar of the engine. He noticed the two pursuing men had guns with them.

"Start moving!" Charlotte ordered him.

Nick obeyed, lining himself up with the short runway. It looked like the angry guard was about to catch up with Bill, who looked at least forty years his senior.

"Bill," Nick yelled to warn him, "behind you!"

The guard came up right behind Bill and lunged at him, sailing through the air with impressive speed for his size. His arms latched onto Bill's ankles, sending Bill crashing to the ground, clods of earth and grass kicking up around them.

Hearing the thud of Bill hurtling to the ground, Charlotte turned and bolted towards Bill, who was trying to kick the hefty man off himself.

Nick angled the plane towards them, reasoning that if he could roll over a few bad guys, his life as a pilot would be complete, and he could proudly include it on his application to be on the MacGyver cast.

Charlotte reached the struggling pair first. She aimed a well-placed kick, which incapacitated the man for a few seconds and caused all the other men to gasp with empathy, involuntary tears springing to their eyes at the imagined pain. Then she hauled Bill up by the arm and dragged him towards the approaching airplane.

By this stage, the second guard had caught up. He stopped, drew his weapon, and tried to steady his arm as he aimed at Charlotte's back.

"Duck!" Nick bellowed.

Charlotte pulled Bill down with her, both flattening themselves on the damp grass as the bullet flew past, clipping the wing of Nick's plane.

"Oh, *now* he's gone too far!" Nick scowled as he changed the plane's direction and zoned in on the guard still trying to take aim.

Too late, the guard noticed the plane bearing down on him and was forced to drop low as it rolled over him, the wheel catching his leg. He howled in agony, causing a sick grin of satisfaction to spread over Nick's face.

"What's wrong with you?" Charlotte grumbled as she shoved Bill into the plane and pulled herself in after him. "You can't drive over innocent people with your plane!"

"I saved your life, you know," Nick pointed out with a scowl. "What's this all about, anyway? That guy was shooting at you!"

Charlotte waved a little black book at him and grinned. "Let's not tell, Olly, okay?"

"No," Bill objected. "No more secrets from Oliver, or anyone. Nick, my name is Malik Bouchard. Pleased to meet you."

"So lovely of you to radio in again," Charlotte answered with a smirk. "How can I help you, Rick?"

"Give it back!" he roared over the crackly line.

"Give what back?" Charlotte asked innocently.

"You have no idea what you've stolen from me, or what I'll do to you to get it back!" Rick spat.

"Actually, my good friend Malik explained exactly how valuable your little book is. Something about all the evidence the police would ever need to send you to prison for as long as scum like you deserves to rot there…"

"Fine," Rick said, surly. "What do you want in return?"

"My children. All four of them."

"I'll have them released. But I want my book first."

"There's no way I trust a single word that comes out of your mouth. First light tomorrow, you arrive here with my children. Once they're safely back in my care, I'll give you your stupid book back, and this all ends here. You leave my family alone forever, and that includes Malik. Got it?"

The radio crackled undisturbed for some time before Rick's voice finally agreed. "Fine."

Charlotte disconnected and let out a long sigh of relief. "He agreed," she repeated for the benefit of the small group squashed into her office.

"I'm going to throttle this Rick with my bare hands when I see him," Alf seethed.

Charlotte managed a small smile. While she felt sick to her stomach that her beloved children would have to fend for themselves overnight, there was now the tiniest flicker of hope that they would resolve everything.

"I'm worried about Lola," Barb said tearfully. "She's not like your children, Charlie. Lola hasn't been toughened up by the untamed wild that surrounds your children daily."

"Thomas will look after them," Charlotte assured. "He's a smart kid in dealing with difficult situations. He'll keep them calm and safe, and make sure they do nothing stupid to get themselves killed. Rick is in our hands now. So all our kids have to do is sit tight and wait for the adults to rescue them."

Barb and Alf nodded appreciatively at Charlotte's words, and Alf slipped an arm around his wife's tiny frame, drawing her closer to comfort her.

Charlotte instinctively turned to look for comfort from her own husband before remembering he still wasn't home.

An observant Malik noticed this and came to her rescue, pulling her into a hug.

***

Thomas pressed his finger across his lips, signaling the three other kids to remain silent while he got up.

Amelia watched him with wide, trust-filled eyes. Meanwhile, Owen was distracted by a moth, and Lola looked terrified.

Denver and Louis had both fallen asleep, curled around the small campfire. Their bulging, shivering bodies were unused to the harsh conditions of camping outdoors next to an enormous body of water that breathed damp, icy air on them all night.

During the long hours of their capture, Owen had squirmed his wriggly fingers out of their ropes—a fact he revealed once the men were sleeping by reaching for an apple. Upon seeing that Owen's hands were free, Thomas immediately tasked the younger boy with freeing the rest of them from their ties, and then scolded him for not doing so sooner.

"Now what?" Lola whispered in Thomas's ear.

"Just follow my lead," he instructed, his eyes lingering on Lola's for a second longer.

He used sign language, which his siblings readily understood, to explain that they were going to steal the boat.

Lola vehemently shook her head, using her own sign language to state that he was insane and the smart thing to do would be to sit and wait for help.

Thomas waved this off and repeated his own plan in hurried flicks of his fingers.

A little stamp of Amelia's foot reminded them they were wasting valuable time. Thus, it was put to the vote, and all except Lola voted in favor of Thomas's plan.

With the democracy of sibling rivalry sufficiently dealt with, the small group tip-toed to the small boat that had brought them. Thomas worked in silence on the knot until the boat tugged away, immediately finding the current and carrying them slowly away from danger. He took a running leap and jumped into the boat, the noise regrettably disturbing Denver.

Denver scrambled up, his eyes alert and his face pale with shock as he watched the four children make off in the boat. He looked down at Louis, strangely hesitating to wake his partner.

Thomas watched with growing curiosity as Denver raised his hand in silence and waved them off with a wide grin on his face. He then observed with equal surprise when Amelia bounced up in the boat and waved to Denver, the silvery moonlight illuminating her beaming smile as they drifted away from the small island.

"What did I miss?" he asked Lola, who shrugged with confusion.

"Uncle Denver is my new best friend," Amelia informed them with a gleeful smile. "We both love unicorns."

"You're crazy," Owen mumbled, still cradling his giant moth.

Thomas glanced back at the island and saw Denver lay back down in his spot by the warm glow of the dying fire. For the millionth time, he thought about how confusing grownups were. Then, shaking the thought away, he handed

Lola one of the free oars and the small group, huddling together for warmth, quietly paddled away in search of something that looked familiar and would signify home.

Chapter 9
Missing Treasure

"He's late," Alf pointed out with a huff.

"Criminals aren't known for their punctuality," Malik retorted.

The group had been snapping and snarling at each other all morning as their patience in waiting for Rick Neilson wore thin.

"Perhaps he was delayed in fetching the kids," Nick suggested.

Charlotte noticed that a very distraught Madison was standing close at Nick's side. While Nick had been trying for the last decade to win over Madison's affections, Madison had wanted nothing to do with him. The smug expression tugging the corners of Nick's mouth up suggested that things had finally changed for him.

Malik shook his head. "Or he's up to something. Rick's not usually late, especially when someone has something he wants."

Charlotte bit her lip nervously. Malik had just voiced her deepest concern, and she worried that the fear would erode the group's courage.

"I have some good news," Madison said, as though she had only just remembered. "I got through to Corporal

Dumont. He apologizes for being delayed, and promises he'll be here later today, weather permitting, of course."

There was a short-lived cheer of relief from the group at the prospect of professional help finally being on the way, but this was soon replaced with the growing dread that Rick would not show up and the whereabouts of their children would be lost with him.

But Rick Neilson showed up.

Alone.

His boat rolled in at the edge of the lake, and the group trotted down to meet him. Every pair of eyes scanned the inside of the boat in shock.

"Where are our children?" Alf demanded.

Rick sneered before looking towards Charlotte. "Who are these idiots?"

"You stole one kid too many. The fourth one belongs to them," she answered quickly, so that Alf did not announce how rich and important he was. She didn't trust Rick to stick to his terms if he knew he could profit from another wealthy family.

"We have a slight problem," Rick mumbled.

"What did you say? Speak up," Alf demanded.

Rick rolled his eyes but obeyed. "We have a problem," he announced, louder.

"I don't want any games, Rick. The corporal is on his way and I'll give him everything in that book."

Rick cringed, which showed to Charlotte that he was telling at least a smidgen of the truth.

"Don't think for a second that you can lure us away from the lodge with a tall tale, just so that some more of your goons can search the property for the book. You won't find it," Malik declared.

"Well, well, Malik," Rick spat, "you've found your voice after all these years of hiding like a coward."

"Enough," Charlotte interrupted. "Where are our children?"

"Come and see for yourself," Rick suggested.

"That wasn't part of the deal."

"Trust me," Rick said with the tiniest shred of sincerity coating his words, "you're going to want to come with me."

Charlotte shot a doubtful look at Malik, who shrugged in return.

"Fine, I'll come," Charlotte agreed. "But any tricks, and that information goes straight to the corporal."

"I'm coming too," Alf asserted.

Malik stepped forward. "Me too."

"So are we!" Madison jumped on board.

"No," Charlotte said, punching the wind out of her sails. "You and Nick stay behind, just in case the corporal arrives while we're gone." Ignoring their downcast expressions, Charlotte climbed into one of her own boats.

Malik and Alf followed behind her. Then Barb clambered in, clutching to the sides uncertainly, her dread of the unknown and icy depths not enough to deter her from rescuing her daughter.

"We could just take one boat," Rick said.

"This isn't some kind of family outing," Charlotte retorted. "You literally stole my children. There's no way I'm catching a free ride with you to find them."

Rick scowled at her before stepping into his own boat and switching on his motor. "I was just trying to be a gentleman."

Charlotte shook her head in disbelief as she revved her engine and pulled up the boat behind him. The two boats charged off, Charlotte closely following Rick.

"Rick's not all bad, you know," Malik whispered.

"Excuse me?" Charlotte fired over the roar of the wind and the two boats.

"Rick used to have a family of his own. Times got hard and his wife walked out on him. I guess he thought that if he could earn enough money, by honest or dishonest means, he might lure her back."

"I can't believe you're defending this guy right now," Charlotte bellowed into the wind.

Malik shrugged. "I'm just saying that people are complex. Rick's ambition in life wasn't to be a villain. He just wanted to support his family."

Charlotte hesitated, wondering if she had lost grip with reason. "But Rick didn't have to go around taking down mines and holding children ransom. That was *his* choice."

"I was once a bad guy too. My motives were like his. It didn't feel like much of a choice."

"You were a desperate man in a critical situation. There's a difference. And I still believe that we always have the choice whether to do right or wrong."

Malik grinned at her and shrugged like a young boy caught stealing cookies out of the jar.

Rick's boat slowed down, and Charlotte decelerated accordingly, her stomach twisting into a knot at what lay ahead. As they rounded the little island, she spotted the familiar thugs she'd encountered at Malik's cabin. Her eyes scanned past them to a small tent that had been erected farther up from the shore. Her heart raced.

"Tom! Owen! Amelia!" she yelled, unable to contain her excitement.

But there was no response. As if in answer to her confusion, the wind caught a flap of the tent, blowing the doorway open and revealing an empty tent, devoid of her children.

Their boats slowed to a stop and Charlotte leapt out into the shallow water. She climbed up onto the island, her rifle ready in case Louis or Denver tried anything.

"Your stupid kids aren't here," Louis informed her between gritted teeth.

"They escaped!" Denver added with excitement.

"I told you we had a problem," Rick said. "Your children ran away in the middle of the night. Your side has breached our agreement."

Charlotte rounded on him. "Are you telling me that two grown brutes capable of killing people, failed to keep an eye on four children all under the age of fifteen?!"

"Calm down, Charlie," Malik counseled quietly.

"How can you kidnap children and then lose them?" she screamed. "You're not laying a finger on your precious book until I have my kids home with me!"

Rick flashed her a scathing look. "Fine," he said after a moment. "We can split up and go out searching by boat."

"Not a chance." Charlotte moved quickly towards Rick's boat and swung one leg inside.

"What do you think you're doing?" he shouted at her.

Charlotte prodded him out of his own boat with the barrel of her gun. "I don't trust you, so you're waiting here," Charlotte announced, kicking the boat into gear, and shooting away from the island.

"You're going to pay for this!"

"No, Rick. *You're* the one who's going to pay for everything you've done!" she yelled over her shoulder.

Malik followed her in the second boat until they were a safe distance away from the shoreline. Then he pulled his boat up next to hers and slowed down. "What's the plan?" he shouted.

"I'm guessing the kids wouldn't have got the boat keys off one of those guys," Charlotte reasoned, her hair blowing in the wind. "So they likely paddled away manually in the cover of darkness."

"All right, so that limits how far they could have gotten."

"Moonlight was good last night, so they would have been able to see where they were going at least," she reasoned, using the raw facts to build up a logical picture.

"But Thomas doesn't know this part of the lake, so I reckon he would have tried to follow the stars toward home," Charlotte continued, trying to step inside her son's mind.

"That's a lot of distance, and we have no way of communicating if one of us finds them," Malik pointed out.

"Right. So let's stay within sight of each other. If you see anything, honk your boat horn. And I'll do the same. Hopefully, they'll hear our engines and come out from hiding."

"Good idea. We'll take the right."

"Charlie," Barb's voice was soft in the wind, "thank you for being so brave. I know we'll find them."

"Yes," Alf added stiffly, as though he was unused to complimenting others. "We wouldn't know how to do this without you and Bill… I mean, Malik."

"Thank you," Charlotte said, touched by their rare moment of humility. "But let's save this for after we bring our children home. Oh, and one more thing. Keep a look out for Oliver too. He's never stayed away this long before. I'm worrying that something happened to him."

Malik nodded gravely, the traces of concern in his eyes mirroring Charlotte's just before he sped off.

Straining her eyes, Charlotte scanned the waters and dots of islands while a pulsating headache began forming in her temples. Now that she was finally alone, she could let loose how she really felt inside. When her hands began slipping on the steering wheel, she tried to wipe the sweat off on her jeans. All the while, she kept her breathing steady, attempting to prevent herself from hyperventilating. Her mind reeled with the awful possibility of never finding her children again… Or worse.

With a shudder, she dragged her mind away from the dark hole it had been spiraling down and closed her eyes for a second. She allowed her thoughts to drift towards her family members who were missing somewhere on their favorite lake. She realized, with core-wrenching pain, that she couldn't exist without them. Her husband, her children, and now Malik, were all a part of her. They made up her daily happiness and there was no future without them in her life.

When she reopened her eyes, she did so with renewed hope and determination. She blinked a few times before her brain communicated to her what she was seeing.

A boat.

One of their older boats. They painted the glossy logo of a rainbow trout leaping out of the water on all their boats. On this one, the logo was faded. But it was still unmistakably there.

She honked her horn, summoning Malik.

As she drew closer, excitement pumped through her veins. But then she realized with disappointment that this boat couldn't possibly contain her children; they'd stolen one of Rick's boats.

"Olly?" she called.

No answer.

Nearing the side of the boat, she spotted her husband's camping gear and fishing rod, but no sign of Oliver himself.

"What did you find?" Malik shouted while slowing to a halt next to her.

"Oliver's boat, but no Oliver." Her voice wobbled from emotion. "I don't understand. It looks like he didn't even set up camp anywhere."

"Let's not jump to conclusions," Malik suggested wisely. "Alf, how good are your boating skills?"

"Fairly good, old chap. Shall I captain Oliver's boat?"

Malik gave Alf the nod of approval and Alf heaved his body into Oliver's boat. Behind the steering wheel with the wind in his hair, he looked like a different man, though his face was still lined with the anxiety for his missing daughter.

Charlotte caught Malik's eye. "I'm worried," she whispered so that Barb wouldn't hear. "Oliver wouldn't leave his boat unattended like this. I'm worried something happened to him."

"Like what?" Malik asked, trying to shrug off her growing anxiety.

"Storms roll in quickly. He could have been hurt or knocked unconscious in his boat." Charlotte's bottom lip trembled at the imagined episodes her mind conjured.

"If that happened, we would have found him here too. Maybe he didn't anchor his boat, and it drifted away from the shore."

"Maybe," Charlotte said weakly.

"The motor is dead," Alf announced, the disappointment clear in his voice.

"Sometimes the older ones get a bit finicky." Charlotte carefully climbed over into her husband's boat and tried all the tricks she knew to get the old motor running. She scratched her chin, surveying the stubborn chunk of metal. "It *is* dead. I wonder if Olly got stuck out here…"

Charlotte's gaze drifted to the bottom of the boat where she noticed some rust-colored liquid smudged on the surface. She stooped down and examined it closer. "Malik, there's blood…"

"Don't panic, Charlie," he warned. "Olly could have cut himself fishing or trying to fix the motor."

"There's a lot of blood." Charlotte's voice shook, her imagination running wild. She began examining the rest of the goods laying scattered haphazardly in the boat. Usually, her husband would have had everything neatly packed away.

She touched a sweater of his and found it was soaking wet. "I'm almost certain yesterday's storm had something to do with this," she said, her face a mask of grave concern.

"Charlie, we're wasting daylight," Malik said. "We need to get going, especially if we have to include Olly in our search as well."

Charlotte nodded, tearing her mind away from another mystery she couldn't reconcile.

Chapter 10
The Hunt

"You can't light a fire," Lola complained. "Those thugs will track the smoke and find us!"

"But we need to eat." Thomas gestured to the few fish he'd caught with the net they had found in the boat. "Besides, my mom might track the smoke too, and that would be great."

"I'm not eating that." Lola folded her arms. "It was alive like, five seconds ago."

Thomas rolled his eyes and sighed.

"Tom makes the best fish on a fire," Amelia said with a loyal grin.

"We don't have any salt or lemon juice. It's savage," Lola objected. "Anyway, I'm not starving." Yet, her stomach betrayed her with a loud growl.

Owen giggled. "Someone has a hungry tiger in her belly."

Amelia snorted. "Maybe that's why she's so grumpy."

The pair dissolved into giggles again, Owen clutching his belly as he laughed.

Lola stomped off in a huff and found a rock to sulk on.

"You two shouldn't give her such a hard time," Thomas scolded. "She's not like us. She's used to fine city food, not eating fish off a stick." He worked on rubbing his two sticks together, determined to prove himself worthy. He was grateful for the many camping trips he'd endured with his father and Bill, where they had forced him to rough it without the usual supplies of luxury camping. His father and Bill had often chatted away merrily, warming their hands and feet over a roaring fire that they'd used matches to light, while they forced Tom to work on his own miserable little fire from scratch.

His father would always say, *"It's good training, son. One day, you'll thank us."*

Then his father would chuckle and slurp on a hot mug of coffee. Thomas had to admit, he'd always hated hearing that line. But he had finally reached the day where he could think of the training with gratitude instead of bitterness. Tears sprang to his eyes as he thought back to those easier times where the lives of so many didn't weigh on his small shoulders.

The smoke from the two sticks burned his eyes, and soon, a spark caught on some dry moss, bursting into a tiny flame that he quickly fed.

"Nice, son," his father mumbled, before choking into a dry cough.

"Dad!" Thomas jumped up, forgetting his fire. "You're awake! How are you feeling?"

"I have a terrible headache," his father groaned.

"You'd lost a lot of blood when we found you," Thomas said in a gentle voice. "I tried to clean you up as best I could."

"Where are we?" Oliver croaked.

"I'm not sure. But I think we're finding our way home. Lola and I were too tired to paddle any farther, so we stopped and get ready for another night out here," Thomas informed his father, finding it strange to be taking the lead. It pained him to see his father so weak. "I'm going to heat some water so I can clean your wound properly."

"Daddy!" Amelia squealed as she stampeded over, dropping the armload of firewood they had sent her to collect.

"Shh! Dad is still feeling sick," Thomas cautioned.

While Amelia was comforting Oliver, Thomas strayed back to his fire. He'd assumed it had blown out, but he found Lola poking twigs and small chunks of dry driftwood into it. "You saved it," he mumbled awkwardly. "Thanks."

After his short time with Lola, it forced him to conclude that he would never understand girls. He finally understood what Bill and his father used to talk about around the fire—how one minute a girl can get you so worked up, and the next, she's as sweet as pie and cooking dinner.

"I'm sorry I gave you a hard time earlier," Lola said. "I forgot that you've got a sick dad to worry about too."

"He'll be fine. My dad is tough." Thomas tried to hide his worry by flashing a proud smile.

"At least your dad cares," Lola muttered. "All my father is interested in is winning his stupid election so he can affect 'change in the world'." She quoted, mimicking Alf's stern voice.

"I bet your dad is out on this lake looking for you right now," Thomas assured her.

"Sometimes, I think my parents would be happier without me in their lives…"

"I think all kids feel that way sometimes," Thomas said. "But our parents love us."

"That's easy for you to say. Your parents are happily married."

"So?"

"You don't have to go through what I went through." Lola folded her arms again.

"I'm not sure if you noticed, but my dad discovered that an old man who'd been working for us is actually my long-lost, dead grandfather. I figured it out a while ago. I mean, if you just look at the two of them next to each other, it's easy to tell they are the same person. Anyway, my dad got really upset and ran away to go camping. Then my grandfather felt like no one loved him, so he also ran away too."

Lola's eyes widened and her lips parted in surprise.

"Yeah, so my family is not as perfect as it seems," Thomas concluded. "Oh, and I forgot to mention that the guys who stole us were actually out to kill my grandfather…"

Lola's delicate eyebrows furrowed with confusion. "I thought they kidnapped us because my dad is so important and they wanted money from him."

"Nope." Thomas shook his head. "My crazy grandfather upset some rich guy who tried to shoot him on our property, and I had to save him. So I think it had something to do with revenge. And since my grandfather wasn't around to steal, they made do with us."

"Your family is worse than mine." Lola laughed. "I'm sorry, that was rude."

Thomas shrugged as he added more wood to the fire. "They're still my family. And even though we usually get things wrong, we still work hard to be there for each other. I wouldn't want to belong to any other family."

"I think I want to be a part of your family too," Lola said with an envious smile.

Thomas blushed.

Unfortunately, Owen had been lying in wait for such an opportunity. "Ooooh, Lola wants to become Lola Bouchard!" he squealed, skipping around them with giddy laughter.

"Owen!" Thomas shouted. "How do you even know about stuff like that?"

Owen continued his relentless torture, which eventually led to Thomas chasing him around the island and waving a piece of driftwood at him.

***

Charlotte had slowed the boat to a stop. She was studying the sky to estimate what the clouds were doing and how much light they had left.

"What are you thinking?" Malik asked.

Charlotte slumped her shoulders in defeat. "It's been *hours*."

"We've still got quite a distance to go. We're cutting it fine if we still want to make it home before dark."

"I can't leave my babies out here alone another night," Charlotte cried, her strength crumbling. With each passing watery mile, her determination and hope had been flushed away, leaving her devoid of anything but dread. "What if—"

"You can't dwell on 'what ifs'," Malik interrupted.

Charlotte nodded, swallowing the lump that threatened to close her throat and render her a useless, emotional wreck. Releasing a slow, long breath, she looked up at Alf and Barb, who'd been watching her closely. "It'll be okay," she assured Barb, using her remaining strength to offer them a reassuring smile. "Our kids couldn't have gotten much farther than this line manually, so they're somewhere close."

Alf held Barb upright. Her eyes were swollen and red, her hair was a mess, and it crinkled her clothes from constantly getting wet and then drying.

Charlotte reached out and took Barb's hand. "We can do this, Barb. We're in this together. And I'm so relieved to have all of you as part of my team."

"Glad to have you on our team too," Alf said, giving Charlotte a nod. "All my life, I've preferred surrounding myself with people who don't give up in the face of defeat, even when outnumbered, and it seems the odds are against you. I couldn't be happier to have found that here and—"

"Shh!" Charlotte held up her hand, silencing Alf.

"Excuse me?"

"Shh," Charlotte said again.

Alf's face reddened.

"I hear giggling," Charlotte explained. "I *know* that giggling!" Her eyes flitted from the island to the rocks and tree, convinced any random object was one of her children.

The group fell into a deadly silence as every ear fought to discern sounds of children over the water lapping against the boat, wind rustling through pine needles, and their own thumping hearts.

A fish eagle cried in the distance.

"Sorry, Charlie, but I think you're hearing–"

"Wait," Charlotte signaled for silence again.

This time they all heard the piercing shriek of laughter.

Malik and Charlotte exchanged a hopeful look.

"That's Owen!" Charlotte screamed, her eyes flooding with tears of joy.

"There!" Malik pointed to the sky.

They had missed the thin trail of white smoke drifting up from a tiny island in the distance.

Charlotte's hands shook as she started up her boat and spurred across the water towards the small island. As it ranged into view, she could hardly believe her eyes as the tiny figures grew into the familiar shapes and smiles of her children.

Charlotte barely felt the cold water as it slurped into her boots and splashed up her front. She hurdled through the water until she tripped her way up the rocky shore and collapsed on her knees in front of the startled little group.

Amelia reached her first, shooting into her arms with a force that nearly knocked her over. Owen was next. He gripped Charlotte around her neck so tightly, he choked the air out of her.

"You're going to kill Mom," Thomas scolded Owen.

"Come here, you," Charlotte spluttered in between sobs.

"Tom went all *Lord of the Flies* on us!" Owen complained.

Charlotte's strong fourteen-year-old son dissolve into tears of relief as he dropped to his knees and buried his face in her neck. "I'm so glad you found us," he whispered in her ear.

"You saved us, Mommy," Amelia wailed.

"No!" Owen protested indignantly. "Thomas saved us before he turned all savage!"

Charlotte squeezed her beautiful children tighter. Over Owen's bird's nest hairdo, she noticed an uncertain Lola standing alone, her face distraught.

Charlotte had forgotten about Alf and Barb. It would have taken them longer to climb out of the boat and make their way slowly onto the island. She craned her neck backwards and saw them stumbling their way up the incline.

"Lola! Honey!" Barb's frantic voice called.

"Mom?" Lola said, the disbelief written all over her small face. She bolted towards her mother, nearly knocking her off her feet. "I can't believe you came to find me! I thought you didn't care about me!"

Barb's face distorted with pain at her daughter's words. "I had no idea you felt like that…"

Alf finally arrived, spluttering and out of breath. Without hesitation, he drew his wife and daughter into his arms and held them tightly.

"Mom," Thomas called her.

"Yes, love?"

"Dad is really sick."

"What?" Charlotte leapt up.

"We found him in his boat. He hit his head really badly, and he sleeps a lot."

Charlotte ran to their little camp and noticed that what she'd thought was a bundle of rags lying under the tree was actually her husband wrapped in a tattered blanket. "Olly! Love," Charlotte called as she dropped to her knees at his side and caressed his face.

There was a deep purple bruise on the side of his forehead, and a nasty infected-looking cut. "Hey, baby," Olly mumbled, his eyes sunken and his face pale.

"Malik," she shouted over her shoulder, "we need to get Olly home as soon as possible!"

Malik nodded gravely; his dark eyes fixed on Oliver's wan complexion.

"Let's move him," she ordered, swinging one of Oliver's arms around her neck.

After what felt like hours, Charlotte finally recognized their familiar piece of shore in the dim light of waning evening. The crisp air had chilled them to the core. Charlotte's teeth chattered as she stiffly climbed out the boat. "We made it," she said in relief.

Benjamin and Nick were waiting with lanterns. They sprang into action at the sight of the unconscious and injured Oliver, hoisting him up gently and placing him on a plank of wood.

"Get him warm," Charlotte ordered. "I'll need boiling water and my first aid."

The two young men ran up the incline towards the lodge building, disappearing into the darkness. Charlotte waited patiently as her exhausted children stumbled out of the boat, sleepy-eyed.

Alf, Barb, and Lola walked up next, while Charlotte and Malik remained behind to sort out the boats.

"All right," Charlotte said, "let's go home."

"Not so fast," came sinister voice penetrating the darkness.

Charlotte would know that voice anywhere. It had plagued her dreams every night she closed her eyes, and it dominated her waking thoughts in the safety of daylight. "What do you want, Rick?" she said, finding his shadow. She noticed the two larger shadows behind him. Louis and Denver.

"I want what is rightfully mine. My book."

Charlotte pulled it out of her bag and stepped forward to hand it over. "Pleasure doing business with you."

"You had it with you the whole time?" he spat, angered at being outsmarted yet again.

Charlotte shrugged. "Can't be too careful with leaving things lying around. You never know who might steal it. How did you get off the island, anyway? We were going to come fetch you in the morning."

Rick glared at her. "You've pushed me too far, Charlotte Bouchard. I don't enjoy being ordered around by anyone, let alone a woman."

"Look, Rick, it's over now. If you want to take things further, I'll give Corporal Dumont, who's probably walking this way to check on us anyway. A big shout and he can help settle things down. Maybe he can even look at that precious book of yours."

"I've had enough of you." Rick raised his weapon and pointed it squarely at Charlotte.

"Put the gun down," Malik said. "Your original fight was with me."

Charlotte raised her hands in surrender. "You're right," she said in a calm voice, her eyes glued to Rick. "I pushed you too far, and I apologize."

"It's too late for that," Rick yelled. "How dare you think you can stand up against me! You have no idea what I'm capable of!" His usually slick hair was a tousled mess, and his eyes were pinpricks of fury buried deeply in his contorted face. As he shouted at her, tiny flecks of spit flew out of his mouth.

"Rick," Charlotte pleaded, "you don't want our blood on your hands. I know I might seem like a threat to you, but really, I'm no one worth worrying about. All I care is that I have my family safely with me. I've just got them back, so I'm ready to move on. Aren't you? Aren't you ready to walk away from this? You had a family too once, didn't you?"

"You don't get to talk about them!" The whites of his eyes had turned almost ghostly in the pale moonlight.

"What would they say if they could see you now?" she asked quietly.

His gun rattled in his trembling hand.

"This isn't you, Rick," Charlotte continued. "You're a man who cared about your family once. Go find them. Bring some peace and happiness into your life for a change. If you kill me, you'll never find peace again. You'll be hunted down until you're caught and thrown into prison for the rest of your life. You have a chance to do what's right, but it's your choice."

Rick absorbed her words slowly, his manic stare softening and getting replaced with sorrow. He swallowed, his hand wavering. Slowly, he lowered his weapon.

"Thank you," Charlotte said.

Louis couldn't bear being outsmarted by Charlotte Bouchard again. He lunged forward to grab the gun away from Rick and finish the job himself. In one swift motion, Louis raised the gun and fired at Charlotte.

She screamed, clutching her stomach and waiting for warm blood to fill her hands. Her only thought was feeling comfort at knowing she would at least die protecting her family.

But Charlotte Bouchard wasn't dying.

She gasped in relief, stunned as she looked down to examine the wound that didn't exist. In the darkness, she saw a figure drop to the ground in front of her. "Malik!" she screamed, rushing towards his dark silhouette on the ground. "What did you do?" she scolded, rolling him over. Her fingers felt a warm, wet substance seeping through his clothing. "Stay with me. Please, I can't lose you again…"

"What have you done, you idiot!" Rick yelled at Louis. "Now we have blood on our hands!"

"You said you wanted Malik taken care of, whether or not we got the book back," Louis argued.

"Yeah, but I meant quietly, when no one was around to report it to the Mounties!"

"We have no choice but to kill her too, boss. No witnesses."

Louis raised the weapon at Charlotte again as she knelt over Malik.

She took a deep breath, closed her eyes, and prepared for the worst. Again. It was rather a raw deal, having to prepare herself to die for her family twice within ten minutes.

The gun fired a second time, this time overshooting into the tree branches above her head.

Confused, and certain that she hadn't been hit this time, Charlotte opened her eyes and saw Louis passed out in the dirt. It was hard to tell what had happened in the darkness, but Denver was kicking the gun away from Louis's reach, so she assumed he had come to her rescue. The strange man grinned at her in the moonlight.

The fired shots had brought Nick, Benjamin, and the corporal running from the main lodge. Rick and Denver disappeared into the dark trees, their feet sloshing through water as they tried to make off in a boat.

"Charlie?" Nick's voice called.

"Over here," she yelled back, applying pressure to Malik's wound. "Malik," she pleaded, "please, stay with me. Please, don't leave me. The kids need their grandfather. Olly needs his dad. We all need you."

She felt his fingers grip hers for a moment before losing strength and falling away slack.

Chapter 11
Healing Wounds

"Just eat your soup," Charlotte moaned.

Her husband stared resentfully at his bowl of chicken broth.

"Chef Victor made it just for you," she added.

"I need a proper meal, like steak…"

"Your body is still fighting the infection you got from that awful head wound of yours," Charlotte explained for the tenth time that hour.

Oliver wrinkled his nose at the soup before setting it down next to him. "If I told you what happened, would that earn me a steak? Or at least some chocolate pudding?"

"You *remember*?"

"Yeah, but it's nothing glamorous. I felt like quite the fool when it all came back to me." He chuckled, his hand moving to his recovering wound as a shock of pain went through his head from the laughter.

"So, what happened?" Charlotte asked. She had been waiting patiently for two weeks to hear the tale.

"I was on my way to one of my favorite secret camping spots when the storm rolled in faster than I'd expected. I thought I could just push that last stretch, but you know how the lake gets when those winds pick up and the waves pound on you…"

Charlotte imagined the scene with increasing horror.

"I must have lost my grip of the steering and smacked my head, because that's all I remember until waking up under the tree with Owen prodding at my forehead," Oliver concluded.

"Can we agree on something, my dear husband, whom I love very much?"

"Let me guess. No more secret camping spots that I storm off to when I can't cope with life?"

Charlotte bowed her head. "If you would be so kind." She stood, removed the offending chicken soup, and placed a gentle kiss on his lips. "I love you."

"I love you too," he returned, his hand catching her arm before she left. "I thought I was going to die out there. Freezing. And worst of all, alone. And I had no reason to be there. I had no reason to be alone. I never want to leave you all again, for any reason. From now on, I promise to stay and face the challenges with you. Can you ever forgive me?"

Charlotte swallowed back her emotion and wiped a tear from her cheek before kissing her husband again. "There's nothing to forgive. But I would love to spend the rest of my life with you by my side, instead of waiting for you to come back."

Oliver, who was never very gifted at dealing with emotional moments, wiped away his own tears and sniffled. "Any news about Malik?"

Charlotte shook her head and left the room.

Earlier that night, Nick and Benjamin had performed their stretcher act again, carrying Malik to the house and laying him on one of the dinner tables.

Young Corporal Dumont, who had a higher level of first-aid than Charlotte, retrieved the bullet, with her assistance as a strong-stomached nurse. Madison had attempted to help, but after fainting three times. They dismissed her.

The corporal had stitched up the bullet wound as best he could, satisfied that it had missed all the vital organs. The following morning, at first light, Nick had flown Malik to the hospital along with the corporal and a handcuffed, disgruntled Louis.

They had received no word about Malik since, despite Charlotte radioing the hospital as often as the weather would permit.

The Columbus family bustling towards her disturbed Charlotte's pensive state. Despite the horrendous events of their first few days at the lodge, Alf had extended their stay for an additional two weeks, insisting they needed time to bond as a family.

Thomas and Lola had fought and made up constantly during this time, eventually deciding they could manage being friends. But if anything romantic ever developed, one would have to kill the other.

Barb had learned how to flyfish. Despite her initial fears of almost anything to do with water, fishing, and the outdoors, Barb had proved herself the avid fisher women, surpassing her husband in a matter of days, and even out-fishing Thomas. The four had spent long days out on the waters of Lake Athabasca, picnicking on the islands and cooking fresh fish on a fire that Thomas forced Lola to build herself.

Alf had transformed into a peaceful, jovial man who seized every opportunity to kiss his wife.

"I'm thinking of tossing it all up, Charlie," he announced to her that morning as they met in the hallway.

"Tossing what up?" Charlotte asked, confused. Her thoughts were still on Malik.

"Politics," Alf spat the word.

"Dad is thinking of moving to Canada," Lola explained.

"And how do you feel about that?" Charlotte asked.

"Mom is panicking about the shops and the bears, but I think I prefer it here," Lola stated with approval. "I think we found ourselves as a family."

"I think we did too," Charlotte repeated, giving Lola a smile.

"We're heading out for another fishing exploration," Alf informed. "Only a few days left before we have to return."

Charlotte waved them off at the door. She remained for a while, leaning against the door frame, staring out at the beauty of her surroundings. Her eyes glossed over Malik's cabin and she pushed away the pang she felt creep into her chest. She was just about to return inside, when she spotted a flash of red moving through the trees.

"The corporal is back," she announced excitedly to the house.

Madison immediately jumped into action, organizing a tray of snacks and tea.

Charlotte waited patiently, hoping a second figure would follow the corporal, but he was alone. She bit back her disappointment and walked out to greet him. "It's lovely to have you back, Corporal Dumont."

"Please, Charlie, to you, it's Noah," he stated, as he did every time he arrived.

"I thought you might have brought Malik with you," she pointed out desperately.

The corporal studied her for a second before saying, "Let's go inside and talk, shall we?"

Charlotte nodded sadly.

Charlotte had to shoo away the entire staff and two of her children, who were all eager to glean news of Malik.

"We can chat privately in my office," she said while delivering a threatening glare to the staff as they edged closer.

"Before we do, I just want to let you all know that Malik recovered fully from his injury," Noah announced with a proud grin.

Uproarious cheering erupted from everyone within earshot.

The corporal continued, "They discharged him a few days ago."

This added news was met with confused silence. The staff drifted away slowly, muttering to each other.

"That was strange," Noah commented.

Charlotte closed the door behind them and asked what everyone had been thinking. "If he was discharged a while ago, why didn't he come home?"

"Ah, I see..." Noah nodded. "Well, I have more news. Malik Bouchard asked to see me after he regained consciousness."

Charlotte tried to keep her face neutral.

"He said that he had a confession. Charlie, Malik told me everything. He explained Rick Neilson's involvement in the false testimonies and deaths at the mine. He gave me names. He confessed to being one of those false testimonies and agreed to testify in court."

Charlotte nodded, realizing that a full confession from Malik over not just Rick's heinous crimes, but his own involvement in them too, meant she would likely never again see him without bars obstructing her view. "Is he in jail now?"

"Rick was a big catch for law enforcement. Malik's intimate knowledge of the crimes and the black book which we found on Rick, was invaluable to taking down a criminal who has reigned this area for far too long."

"What does that mean, Noah? What does this mean for Malik?"

"They struck a deal with him." Noah smiled. "The only problem is that Malik's family was paid a substantial amount of money to his fake death. It's a bit hard to let that go. Unless we can figure out how to reconcile that, he may still have to do prison time. The problem is that it would be in the same place as Rick and Louis, and they'll likely take him out in the first week for being a rat."

Charlotte began pacing, her fingers twirling the end of a curl while she thought.

"But don't worry," Noah assured. "I'm working to get him into a different place. Maybe the judge will even bump it down to community service."

Charlotte stopped for a second, a small smile spreading across her lips.

Noah laughed. "Oh, I know that look. You've got something up your sleeve…"

"What if Malik could return the original cheque?" she asked.

Noah scoffed. "That's impossible."

"Not when you have a husband as stubborn as mine. Oliver refused to touch a dime of that money. He called it blood money. It's been sitting in our safe ever since."

The corporal's jaw dropped. "Yeah," he gulped. "That could definitely go a long way. If you have it on hand, I'll get it straight to where it needs to go."

"There's one more thing. Do you have any idea why Malik confessed after all these years?"

Noah nodded slowly and smiled. "He told me a powerful woman reminded him we always have a choice to do right or to do wrong. I guess he finally found the strength to make the right choice."

Charlotte reached for another shirt off her endless pile of clothes needing darning and paused instantly when she recognized it as one of Malik's. She glanced around the room to make sure the kids were asleep before drawing the shirt to her chest and hugging it against her.

"You know, that was the shirt Malik used to wear when he mucked out the horse stables," Oliver commented from behind his book.

"You weren't to see that," Charlotte mumbled.

"I miss him too," Oliver croaked out, his face remaining hidden behind his book.

"I can sense when you're crying," she commented. "There's no point hiding behind Sherlock Holmes."

"How cleverly deduced," he mocked her.

She was about to respond when their banter was interrupted by a knock on the door. Charlotte, assuming it was Madison turning in for the night, climbed off the sofa and swung the door open.

"Hey, Charlie," an old familiar voice greeted her.

Charlotte dove into his arms.

"Careful," the old man coughed. "They shot me saving you, remember?" he teased.

"Dad?" Oliver's voice called.

Malik stepped into the room. He looked as though he had aged a couple of years, and yet, there was a peace about him that Charlotte could only attribute to a clean conscience, and the knowledge that he had a family who loved him.

"Welcome home, old man," she said with a smile.

The End

Now that you have finished this cozy mystery, please consider writing a review on Amazon. It would be appreciated.

* 9 7 9 8 5 9 5 0 8 0 1 7 0 *